1981

A Year in the Life of Nick Taylor

By Jason Ayres

Text copyright © 2024 Jason Ayres
All Rights Reserved

This is a work of fiction. Names, characters, businesses, places, events and incidents are either the products of the author's imagination or used in a fictitious manner. Any resemblance to actual persons, living or dead, or actual events is purely coincidental.

Contents

December 2020 1

January 1981 27

February 1981 56

March 1981 75

April 1981 92

May 1981 107

June 1981 125

July 1981 141

August 1981 160

September 1981 181

October 1981 197

November 1981 214

December 1981 229

January 2021 247

December 2020

"He's still not answering the phone!" I exclaimed, the frustration evident in my voice as I slammed the handset back onto its cradle. It was the third time that morning my father had failed to pick up. "This isn't like him."

"Have you tried his mobile?" suggested Thomas Scott, my colleague and friend from the other side of our large open-plan office. We'd known each other for nearly thirty years, our friendship forged in the aisles of the supermarket where we worked in our early twenties. It marked the beginning of a flourishing career in retail for both of us.

"He's eighty-two years old and he never goes out," I replied. "Especially since this Covid business started. He's classed as a vulnerable person and doesn't want to take any chances. He won't even take a delivery without having it disinfected first."

"He's not the only one," said Thomas. "I mean, look at this place."

I cast my eyes around the room. This was the buying department of one of the largest food retailers in Britain. Roughly the size of a tennis court, the room accommodated around thirty people on a busy day, the office buzzing with activity as they went about their business. Today it seemed vast and empty with Thomas and me being the only two occupants in the brightly lit space. Desks were empty, chairs unoccupied, and it was eerily quiet.

It wasn't unusual for the office to be quiet at this time of year. We were in that strange week between Christmas and New Year when most businesses only keep a handful of staff on duty. But this year the situation was exacerbated by the pandemic's impact. Since the advent of the coronavirus earlier in the year, most of the office staff had taken to spending the majority of their time working from home.

This was in stark contrast to those hardy souls, paid far less than us, who had been keeping the stores running during the crisis. There had been no isolating or furlough for them. Instead, they had been run off their feet keeping the stores stocked, not helped by panicked shoppers fighting over everything from jars of beetroot to toilet rolls.

"Well, I think something's happened to him," I ventured, just sensing, deep down, that things weren't right. There was a gnawing sense of unease right in the pit of my stomach as if a starving rodent had found its way inside and was munching its way through my innards. I could only remember feeling like this once before and that was on the night my mother had died, almost forty years ago.

The same sensation had gripped me the moment her plane had plummeted into the depths of the Atlantic, even though I couldn't possibly have known it was happening. Many brush off such experiences as superstition, but I know what I felt. Over the years, I'd read enough accounts echoing my own to suggest that there was a kind of sixth sense at work in some people. And that was why I was so worried now.

"You know I have an inkling you may be right," said Thomas gently. "I think you should go and check on him."

"Now?" I questioned. Far from reassuring me, his agreement merely added to my growing sense of unease. Experience had taught me that when Thomas said he had an inkling, it was well worth paying attention.

"Why not? There's only the two of us here, so who's to care? It's not like there's much happening today. I'm thinking of knocking off early myself. It is New Year's Eve, after all. I want to get back to Sarah and Stacey."

It made sense, and given his uncanny ability to predict things with unerring accuracy, I knew I had to go. If Thomas thought there was something to worry about then that was reason enough to act. It was nearly midday so I decided to take an early lunch, drive over to the village, and check on my father.

I took my leave of Thomas, grabbed my jacket and headed out of the room, making for the stairs that led down to the staff entrance at the rear of the building. Unlike the grandiose reception reserved for visitors, this area was spartan. We called it the tradesmen's entrance but it had more of a military feel about it, largely due to the presence of the fierce security guard, former army officer Barry.

After a few years working in London, Barry had recently returned to his old job here in Oxford, and it hadn't taken him long to reacquaint himself with his surroundings. He knew the staff roster inside out and took great pleasure in pointing out the shortcomings of each employee at every opportunity. He was the antithesis of politically correct, which some days was amusing, but I wasn't in the mood for his banter today. I hoped he might be in his back office, gorging himself on tea and biscuits as was often the case. Then I would be able to slip by unnoticed, but no such luck.

"Hold it right there, Taylor," he barked in a voice that never failed to make people obey. He hadn't been a sergeant major for nothing. "Where's your mask?"

"Oh, sorry," I said, remembering what a stickler Barry was for the Covid rules. "There was only me and Thomas in the office, and we were sitting thirty feet away from each other, so we thought it was OK to take them off."

"Did you now? Scott's idea, was it? What have I told you about him, eh? You can tell a lot about a man by the state of his car, do you know that? Well, you should go and have a look at his. Filthy it is, inside and out."

"Yes, well, I'm sorry, Barry, I'll put it back on when I come back," I conceded, heading for the double doors, and hitting the release button. But it didn't work.

"Not so fast, young man."

"Young man? That's very kind of you but I am fifty, you know."

"You're younger than me, so you're a young man. And that means I'm your elder, doesn't it? And how do we treat our elders?"

I sighed, and answered, "With respect," through gritted teeth. I did not disagree with the concept of automatically treating elders with respect just because they were older. It was one of the founding principles on which polite society was based, but it was difficult to justify sometimes.

His words brought back memories of some of my old aunts and uncles, obnoxious individuals who demanded respect they didn't deserve. Then there were the sadistic teachers at the school I had been sent to at the age of eleven. They gloried in the power they had over the boys, and in certain cases, abused it. Perhaps that was one of the reasons I resented authority so much. And right now, when I urgently needed to get out of the building, I had no time for Barry's silly games.

"Right, lad, with respect. So show me some respect, put your mask on, and then I'll let you out. It's the rules."

"But I'm going outside."

"Yes, but you're not out there yet, are you?"

"I would have been if you had let me. So what are you suggesting here? I put my mask on, walk two steps to the door, go outside, and then take it off again?"

"Precisely," replied Barry. "If I let you off, then I'll be setting a precedent, won't I? Give people an inch and they'll take a mile. I should know. I used to work for a national radio station in London, and the big-name presenters were always trying to flout the rules, just because they were famous. So when I came back here, I decided from day one that I would be operating a zero-tolerance policy. I'm not having any of that nonsense here."

"Fine," I said, rolling my eyes as I pulled a disposable blue surgical mask from my pocket and began to loop it over my ears. I did not have the energy for an argument or to listen to one of Barry's long-winded anecdotes about his previous employment, or his time in the military. I had a pressing need to go and find out what had happened to my father so I would just have to play along until he relented and let me out.

"Where are you going, anyway?" asked Barry. "You can't be going out for lunch. I'm sure you must know that all the pubs are shut. We're in tier three."

"Whatever that means," I replied. "I don't know how you keep up with all these rules. They seem to change nearly every day. If you must know, I'm going to check on a family member, that's all."

"Whilst following social distancing guidelines, I trust?"

"Of course," I replied, trying to sound sincere whilst wishing the man would just shut up. "Can I go now, please?"

"Hand sanitiser?" enquired Barry, gesturing at the recently installed dispensers on the wall.

I complied, and finally he let me out. As soon as I was through the door I turned around and made a big show of taking the mask back off. Then I made my way to the near-deserted car park. Less than a year ago, it was a struggle to find a space in the mornings but not anymore. It was cold and clear, and I could feel the chill on my face within a few paces. The weak December sun was doing its best to warm my skin but being so low in the sky, it was woefully ineffective. I hated British winters and wished I could fly off somewhere warm but that wasn't allowed anymore either because of the restrictions.

I got into the company Volvo, a recently acquired hybrid, and made my way out of the building, noting to my relief that the exit barrier was already up. That spared me having to buzz Barry and endure any further lengthy negotiations. Moments later I was turning out onto the ring road.

At least with everyone working from home, there was almost no traffic on the roads. It was scant consolation for the loneliness of the past nine months. It was a close contender for the worst year of my life. I lived on my own with two marriages behind me, neither of which had produced any children. I had always wanted kids but it was beginning to look unlikely, particularly since I had no girlfriend and little prospect of ever getting one under the current circumstances. I had spent most evenings during the lockdowns stuck at home on my own.

There was only one year that had been worse than 2020 and that had been 1981, a time in my life I could barely bring myself to think about. I had spent a lifetime trying to blot the bad memories out but today that was going to be impossible. I was going back to my childhood home, the place where much of the bad stuff had happened. I didn't visit that often because it had been made clear by my stepmother that I wasn't welcome.

My father lived in Wisteria Cottage, the last of a row of five dwellings on the outskirts of a large village a few miles outside Oxford. Most of the other cottages were occupied by wealthy London commuters who had bought them up, modernised them, and now used them as weekend homes.

I didn't know who any of these people were and neither did my father, who said they kept themselves to themselves. He only knew they were from London courtesy of the snooping of Brenda, a nosey neighbour, who had relayed this information to him. Hers was the only other cottage still owned by one of the locals and she had lived there my entire life.

Beyond my father's cottage lay the Meadowbrook Retirement Home. This was an exclusive and upmarket place for well-heeled senior citizens, behind wrought iron black gates and high fences. During my childhood, it had all been very different.

When I was growing up, it was Meadowbrook Farm, the home of my maternal grandparents and the Cartwright family seat for at least two hundred years. My mother, Mary, was the youngest of the four Cartwright children. She had grown up there before she married my father, and they moved into the end cottage.

Three of the cottages were occupied by members of the family back then. They were the final generation from an era when most people didn't move far from their place of birth. Families lived in close-knit communities, the bonds of which had formed over many decades or even centuries. But in forty short years, that way of life had disappeared.

Sometimes I looked back on those childhood times with nostalgia, at least before the point where it began to unravel. But even before my mother died, it wasn't all good. While living in the bosom of one's family had its advantages, it could be stifling too when everybody knew everybody else's business and everyone was expected to know their place in the hierarchy. Which in my case was right at the bottom.

I have heard it said that the past is another country, and it certainly feels like that when I think back to that long-gone world. Society had changed more in my short time on Earth than at any other time in recorded history. Why did it all change? Transport, communication, and technology had all played a part in reshaping the wider world, but with our family, there was more to it than that. The events of that painful year, just under forty years ago, devastated our sleepy little lane, and the fallout drove our community apart. Things were never the same again, and I'm sorry to say that my father, the man I was on my way to see, was one of the key architects of that demise.

Did I hate him for what he had done? It was a real body blow at the time and there was nothing I could do about it. With my mother dead, I was left with only one parent and who else was going to look after me? I could have moved in with my grandparents in the farmhouse but they were elderly by then and it would have been too much for them. All I could do was stay put, unlike my sister Linda who disowned him. She was nineteen and away at university by then, so she was able to take that stance. Before long, she met some rich tosser and washed her hands of both of us. I haven't spoken to her for years, and the last I heard of her was that she was living in Dubai.

Meadowbrook Lane, as the name suggested, ran alongside the brook that gave it its name. It wasn't a very active brook most of the time, just trickling down the left side of the long gravel drive as you looked down the lane from the farmhouse. The lane was about two hundred yards long from there to the junction with the main road at the other end. The only time the brook got lively was after periods of heavy rain. I remember it flooding a couple of times, the water coming over the drive and threatening the cottages, all of which were on the opposite side of the drive. But it always stopped short of flooding us out.

The lane, which gently curved to the left, looked much as it always had but the surrounding land was very different. The fields and woods that had been so full of adventure in my formative years were mostly gone now, replaced by ugly new housing estates.

Back then I knew everyone who lived in each cottage. Now, other than Brenda, I hadn't a clue. As I turned into the lane and drove past the first three, I could see that they had all been extensively refurbished and extended in recent years. I noted at least a quarter of a million quid's worth of cars parked outside, all with 20 or 70 numberplates, which meant they were less than a year old. It was exactly what you would expect to find outside second homes for wealthy commuters.

At least they hadn't changed the traditional names of the cottages. I knew them by heart and as I drove slowly past, tyres crunching on the gravel, the ghosts of the past floated through my mind. First up was Rosemary Cottage, home of the dreaded Aunt Edith, who was unbelievably mean with money. We never called it Rosemary Cottage, though, it was only ever referred to as just Rosemary. That naming convention went for all the cottages.

Next to Rosemary was Fuchsia, Uncle William's former home, where he had lived with his wife, Auntie Jackie, and their daughter, Tracy.

I liked William and Jackie but the thought of Tracy made me incandescent. What went on in that devastating summer of 1981 would have rivalled the storyline of any soap opera, and she was cast in a starring role. It's hard to know where to start when describing her. Back then she was just my cousin but now she is also my stepmother. If that sounds incestuous, it's not, because she and my father aren't blood relatives but given the scandal they caused at the time, they might as well have been.

The middle cottage was Honeysuckle, the former home of the grumpiest pair of old gits I have encountered in my entire life. Edna and Stan hated kids, which wasn't good news for them when a gang of tearaway ten-year-olds were making mischief in the neighbourhood. I swear Stan, or Old Gitface as he was known, would have killed us if he had got his hands on us. His face used to go a furious purple shade when he was coming after us. Perhaps it was no surprise that it was a heart attack that got him in the end. Goodness knows what the old bugger's blood pressure must have been like.

Next came Sunflower, home of the Foster family, and our next-door neighbours. They were not relatives but acted as if they were. Unlike the first three cottages which had been done up in recent years, this one was falling into disrepair, particularly around the roof area where birds or rodents had ripped holes in the eaves. This cottage was one of the few surviving links to my childhood world as it was the home of the ageing Brenda, long a widow, who lived there on her own. She was a lone constant in a world of change but not a welcome one. As I drove past, I saw that true to form, she was in her usual spot.

Whether it was 1975, 1995, or 2020, there was one thing you could guarantee whenever you passed

Sunflower. The blinds on the windows would be twitching as Brenda, the nosiest parker in the history of the world, would have the end of her lengthy nose poking between two of the slats.

This was her favourite vantage point for keeping her beady eyes on proceedings in the lane which, because of its curving nature, enabled her to see the front of all the other cottages. When she wasn't watching from the window she was out in the lane gossiping, most of which was utter horse shit. Her daughter, who thankfully no longer lived there, had inherited this trait and when I was growing up they would often hover like witches in the lane, ready to pounce on the unwary. It was fortunate for them that they had been born in an enlightened period because in medieval times they would have been prime candidates for burning at the stake.

I parked up outside the house where I had grown up with my mother, father, and sister. Now, only he remained, and it was barely his house anymore. Tracy had well and truly taken over, particularly in recent years as old age had begun to take its toll on him. He was almost a quarter of a century her senior. I hadn't been here for a while as Tracy didn't want me there and barely tolerated my weekly phone calls. But someone had to look out for him because I wouldn't have put it past her to neglect him. I had a strong suspicion that she did not care about him anymore and perhaps hadn't for a long time.

His battered old Vauxhall Cavalier was in its usual place on the drive, looking rather forlorn, covered in bird shit and fallen leaves. It looked as if it hadn't moved for a while. Was he even still driving? I pulled in beside it, then went to knock on the front door. In past years I used to let myself in but that was before Tracy changed the locks, another hint that my presence was surplus to requirements. There was no answer, increasing my sense that something was wrong, so I tried the door but it was locked. Then I heard the dreaded, high-pitched voice of Brenda behind me.

"You won't find him in there," she said, having taken her nose out from behind the blinds and come out to investigate what was happening. "And you shouldn't be here. It's the rules."

I turned to see her standing about ten yards away, warily keeping her distance, with her face mask in place. At least this meant I'd be spared the sight of her crooked nose, which last time I had seen it was beginning to resemble a ski-jump. I wouldn't normally mock someone's physical characteristics, either openly or in my private thoughts, but in the case of Brenda she had such a vile personality that I had no qualms about it.

Technically, if I understood the current regulations correctly, she was right that I ought not to be here. Knowing Brenda as I did, I wouldn't have put it past her to report me to the police.

"That's OK," I said, thinking on my feet. "I'm in his bubble."

"Well, I don't know why you've come here, spreading your germs. I thought you would have known. He's at the hospital."

"No, I didn't know," I replied, annoyed not only at the suggestion that I was some sort of plague carrier but also because it was clear that Tracy deliberately hadn't told me.

"In a bad way, he was. Took him away in an ambulance, they did. I said to my Karen on the telephone, that'll be the Covid, that will. Rife, it is. Ambulances going up and down to the care home all the time. Dropping like flies, they are. And I heard that old Mrs Gittins from the flower shop is in a bad way. Such a shame, she only had that new hip last year. And…"

Bloody hell, the woman just went on and on and on. It seemed like she had been doing it my whole life and there was no escape from it. If I didn't interrupt her, I'd be here until midnight, and I had no desire to see the New Year in with her.

"Thank you, Brenda," I said firmly. "Do you know where they took him?"

"The John Radcliffe, I think. I overheard the ambulance men talking as they were loading him in."

"Of course you did. Best I get myself up there, then."

I returned to my car and drove back down the lane, noting that Brenda had gone back inside but I could still see the end of her nose poking out between the blinds as I passed. Then I drove to Oxford and up to the hospital where I had been born.

For once, I had the rare luxury of finding a parking space right away. They were like gold dust at that hospital. It was only after I got out of the car that I wondered how I was going to find him. The John Radcliffe was a vast, sprawling complex built on the side of a hill, with so many levels it was difficult to know where to start. I tried phoning Tracy on her mobile but unsurprisingly, there was no response. She never answered calls from me, and I suspected she had long ago blocked my number. Never mind, I would just have to go to the main reception and ask.

It was only when I got to the main entrance that I realised how difficult this was going to be. There were emergency regulations highlighted in large posters on the entrance which made it clear in no uncertain terms that unless it was essential to be on the premises, visitors were not welcome. That explained the ease of finding a car parking space.

Donning a mask to gain entry, I made my way to the reception desk to enquire about my father but got little joy. I managed to establish that he was in the hospital but I was firmly informed that I would be permitted to go no further. Then, as I was pondering my options, I realised I wouldn't have to.

Turning away from reception empty-handed, I spotted Tracy descending the staircase in front of me, keeping strictly to the right-hand side following the markings on the floor.

My fifty-seven-year-old cousin and stepmother was wearing an expensive cashmere coat, and even at this distance, I could see she was heavily made up. Her dark hair was neatly coiffed and I could see that her nails were impeccably manicured, their bright red shade matching her coat. It was surprisingly out of character for her to look so glamorous as her appearance was normally rather drab. It was as if she had just been on one of those makeover television shows. Who went to that much effort just for a trip to the hospital?

It wasn't just her attire that was different to normal, it was her whole demeanour. She was practically bouncing down the stairs with a spring in her step, and if I could see behind her mask, I expect I would find her beaming away. I could see it in her eyes. Initially, I felt this was promising. If she was this happy then it probably meant my dad was OK.

Her good mood evaporated the instant she clapped eyes on me. I had got used to detecting people's emotions behind their face masks and could imagine the scowl even if I couldn't see it.

"What are you doing here?" she spat out venomously, as I walked across the floor towards her.

"I came to see Dad," I replied before a muscular, bearded security guard interrupted.

"Oi! Social distancing!" he bellowed. "Outside, now!"

"We'll talk outside," I said, as the guard ushered us, at a safe distance of two metres, out of the doors.

"Sorry, but it's the rules," he said, shutting the door firmly behind us. It was the third time today somebody had used that expression on me and I was getting a tad fed up with hearing it.

"Like I said, I came to find Dad," I said, whipping off my mask now we were out in the fresh air. "If it hadn't been for Brenda I wouldn't have even known he was in here. You should have called me."

"Trust that nosey old cow to spill the beans but there was no point in you coming here because you wouldn't have been allowed in any case," she said, keeping her mask on, even though we were now outside. It gave the distinct impression she had something to hide. "They're only allowing one visitor per patient, and only then under exceptional circumstances."

"Such as what?" I asked.

"Like to say goodbye," she replied.

A feeling of dread came over me as I realised what she meant.

"You mean…" I said, my voice tailing off, unable to bring myself to say the words.

"Yes, he's gone."

"Was it Covid?" I replied, noting that she hadn't said sorry or shown any sort of sympathy whatsoever.

"No, he had a heart attack. Two nights ago. I called an ambulance, and they managed to keep him alive but the damage was too much for him at his age. He slipped away about an hour ago."

"And you couldn't be bothered to tell me?" I almost shouted, a mixture of grief at his death and anger at her attitude leading to my raised voice as the emotions threatened to overwhelm me.

"Like I said, you wouldn't been allowed in anyway, so why bother?" she said aloofly, pulling back her sleeve and looking at what to me looked suspiciously like a Rolex.

Caught in a whirlwind of emotions as I was, it didn't stop me from wondering about this and her luxurious coat. Where was all her money coming from? Then I thought about her descending the stairs, full of the joys of spring.

"You don't seem particularly cut up about it," I stated, fighting to hold back the tears as I tried not to be overwhelmed by the enormity of the situation. The last thing I wanted to do was show weakness in front of her.

"He had his time," she said callously. "But life goes on."

"So what happens now?" I asked, thinking about everything that would need to be done. "I mean, there's the funeral, and the house..."

"Oh, you don't need to worry about any of that," she said, "It's all taken care of."

"Yes, but..." I said, fearing the worst. Knowing what a money-grabbing bitch Tracy was I felt I had to find out where I stood, I asked, "...what about the will?"

"Oh, that's something else you don't need to bother yourself about. He changed it a while back, with my help of course. If you were thinking of getting your hands on the family fortune, what little of it there is left, forget it. He's left the lot to me, Kevin, and Andrew."

She was talking about my half-brothers, the two additional children my dad had fathered with her. They hadn't had anything to do with me for years. Tracy had successfully poisoned their minds against me while they were growing up.

"You can't do that," I said, aghast at the unfairness of it all. I had never been lucky with money, as a series of bad investments and my two divorces had left me with very little to show for my fifty years, despite having a good job. While the thorny question of inheritance had never concerned me that much, it seemed harsh that I would not be getting a penny from the home that had initially belonged to my mother and had been part of the family dynasty for generations. Even if Tracy was herself a descendant of that family.

"I think you'll find it's all legal and above board," she said. "So, after the funeral, there's no need for you and me to have any further contact with each other."

The whole time we had been talking she had been casting her eye over my shoulder at the road beyond, and now I discovered why. On the road behind us, on the double-red lines on which no stopping was permitted at any time, a silver two-seater Lotus had pulled up and the driver was honking eagerly on the horn. I had the oddest feeling I had seen the car before but couldn't recall where.

"Oh, here's my lift, must dash," she said, her eyes lighting up with excitement.

She walked over to the car, got in, and made a big show of leaning over to the driver and snogging the face off him, which was clearly for my benefit. No wonder she wasn't bothered about my dad's death or about how I felt. She was all sorted already, and it was then that I remembered where I had seen the car before. It had been parked outside Honeysuckle when I had driven up Meadowbrook Lane earlier.

So she had done it again. As a precocious teenager, she had seduced my father, and now she had got her claws into some rich twat of a neighbour who was quite happy to stop on the red lines. I watched as an ambulance which had just raced in, lights blazing, found him blocking its access.

No doubt it was he who had lavished the coat and the Rolex on her. I was surprised Brenda hadn't said anything about it. If they had managed to sneak around the lane and hide their affair from her, they must have been extraordinarily careful. But with my father gone now, they would have no further need for discretion.

I watched the car roar off as the driver, who I hadn't got a proper look at, went through the gears as if he was on the starting grid at Brands Hatch. Then he almost knocked over a pensioner as he sped over a zebra crossing. The man was without doubt a bell-end of the first order. I stood for a moment, allowing the grief to flow over me now that she was out of sight. It wasn't just his death I was upset about but all the wasted years that had preceded it. I felt the tears welling up but before they could drip down my face, I heard a strangely familiar voice behind me.

"Sounds like you've had a bit of bad luck there, my old son," said the man, in a strong cockney accent. I turned and recognised him straight away. By that, I mean I knew his face and his voice because I had seen him on TV, however his name temporarily escaped me. He went by some sort of nickname, and I scrabbled around in my head trying to retrieve it. How long had he been standing there and how much of the previous conversation had he overheard?

"Oh, er, hello," I said, stumbling a bit. Given my dad's death, and the unpleasant encounter with Tracy, it was no surprise I was not quite with it. "You're that bloke off the telly, aren't you? The Golden Geezer or something?"

"The Diamond Geezer," he corrected me, in an annoyed tone. "But you can call me Keith."

"Of course, Keith Diamond," I said, now my memory had been jogged. "What brings you here? Is it a story about the hospital? I'm afraid I'm not feeling up to being interviewed if that's what you want. My father has just died."

"I'm sorry to hear that, err…" said Keith, leaving the sentence hanging as he allowed me to introduce myself.

"Nick," I replied. "Nick Taylor."

"Well, Nick Taylor, to quote the late great Eamonn Andrews, this is your life. Sorry, I've been dying to say that. Perhaps I should have brought a big red book with me."

He wasn't making much sense but whatever he was here for it didn't seem to have anything to do with the television. There was no film crew or anyone else around. He was on his own.

"I don't understand," I replied weakly. "What are you talking about?"

"Let me put it another way. Perhaps I should have said this is a bit of your life. Specifically, how would you like to spend a year in 1981?"

"I would bloody hate it. It was the worst year of my life. I was sent to a school that I despised, my mother died in a plane crash, and my father had an affair with my cousin. She was the woman that just left, in case you were wondering."

"Keep it in the family, eh?" said Keith. "I don't know, you country folk."

"They weren't blood relatives," I added, knowing what he was implying. It was a conclusion the few people I had confided in about it always jumped to.

"Sounds like it was a bit of an annus horribilis, as Her Majesty, gawd bless her, once said," replied Keith. "But suppose those events weren't necessarily set in stone? What if I told you that you could go back and maybe if it's meant to be, make things turn out differently?"

"I'd say you've got a very vivid imagination. Or you're mentally ill."

"I'm sure you would. I said as much to the woman who sent me back in time. Look, rather than stand around talking for hours, perhaps we should cut to the chase. Hold out your arm."

He reached out his left arm towards me, as if wanting to shake hands but with the wrong hand.

"What about social distancing?" I asked.

"Fuck social distancing," he said. "Just do it."

I felt curiously compelled to comply and then the strangest thing happened. As soon as our hands touched, a golden bracelet with a bright green jewel in the centre materialised on his wrist, and then in lightning-fast time detached itself and wrapped itself around my own. The whole process took a couple of seconds at most.

"There," said Keith. "Better?"

"Not really," I said, wondering what this thing was. There was something odd about it – electronic perhaps? I could sense it throbbing with power but not just in my arm. It was almost as if it were reaching into my mind. "What the hell just happened?"

"Yeah, that's kind of how I reacted when it happened to me," said Keith. "The truth of the matter is that you are now custodian of the timeline."

"That sounds rather important," I said.

"It is," said Keith. "With that bracelet comes great responsibility. At midnight tonight, you're going back to spend a year in 1981."

Under any other circumstances, I would have decried this statement as bullshit but somehow the bracelet's presence made me believe him. I looked at the green jewel pulsing and somehow knew that it was sentient. This thing was alive and it was merging with me.

"Why?" I asked. "I mean, why me?"

"No one knows. I don't know why I was chosen when I spent the year in 1980 but believe me it's an amazing experience. It's changed my whole life."

"You changed history?" I asked. "I thought that was frowned upon. It is in all the time travel films."

"Only if the bracelet approves it. Sometimes you can change things, sometimes you can't. You'll figure it out. And other times you'll be preventing things from happening. I stopped a nuclear bomb going off in London, would you believe?"

"But where am I going to be? How am I going to live? And won't people wonder what this futuristic device is on my wrist?"

23

"Ah, yes, I should have clarified that. You'll be back in your body, as you were in 1981. That's one of the bonuses. I was only twenty-two back then. And I made the most of it if you catch my drift. Oh, and don't worry about the bracelet. It's invisible to everyone but you."

"Yes, but in 1981 I was only ten!" I exclaimed. "How am I going to be able to stop nuclear bombs and stuff at that age? I only got a pound a week pocket money and I had to be in bed by 8pm. I'm not going to have the freedom to do the things you could, am I?"

"Good point. Where were you living in 1981?"

"In a village, not far from here,"

"I'm guessing nuclear bombs weren't on the agenda, then. But the bracelet always selects people for a reason. It chose me and it chose you. It will find things for you to do."

"How did it find me?"

"It guided me here to find you. You'll be doing the same after you get back when you pass it on to the next person. But don't worry about that now, just concentrate on 1981. The best thing you can do right now is go home and cram every bit of information you can lay your hands on about that year into your mind. That's what I should have done before I went back but instead, I spent all day in the pub."

"There's no chance of me doing that," I replied. "They're all shut. Apart from one on the Isles of Scilly, I think. It's the only place in the British Isles still in tier one."

"Crazy," said Keith "Do you have to order a scotch egg? We're going to be talking about all this on the show tonight. Speaking of which, I've got to get back to London. Me and Jimmy are on live from 10pm until after midnight. You should watch if you're not too busy swotting up on 1981. It'll be much better than the Hootenanny or whatever other rubbish the main channels are putting out."

"Maybe I will," I said. Keith's particular brand of reactionary broadcasting wasn't my thing, but he was right about one thing. There was bugger all else on.

"Good man," said Keith. "And I'll tell you one good thing about going back to 1981. The telly's a lot better. And the music. In between saving the world, you'll have a whale of a time. Just let the bracelet guide you and you'll be fine. But don't let it boss you about too much. It can be a fussy little thing. Every time I lit up a ciggie it told me off. But since you're only going to be ten, I guess that won't be a problem. You hadn't started smoking by then, had you?"

"I never did," I replied. "Thank you, Keith."

"You're welcome," he said. "Get in touch when you get back and let me know how you got on, won't you?"

"I will," I promised. There was a lot more I wanted to ask him but he was eager to get off so I let him go and went back to my rented flat in Marston. There, I followed his advice and memorised as much as I could about 1981, looking up everything from pop charts to the winners of major sporting events.

I also gave a great deal of consideration to all the things that had happened in my personal life that year. The more I thought about it the more I realised what an opportunity this was to make a real difference.

Then, at 10pm, I tuned into ChatTV to watch Keith and Jimmy but I couldn't concentrate and my mind kept wandering. I was too preoccupied thinking about the past, which if Keith was right, I would soon once again be a part of.

Could I change things for the better? Would I even be allowed to? The answers to those questions lay forty years in the past and as midnight approached, I was on tenterhooks as I prepared to dive headfirst into the swirling currents of time.

January 1981

"You're alive!" I exclaimed, racing into the kitchen to wrap my arms around my mother.

"Nick darling, why wouldn't I be?" she asked, returning the hug, and running her fingers through my long dark locks. I had hair! A lot of hair! I wasn't completely bald in the future but like a lot of middle-aged chaps, I kept it cropped short to draw attention away from a receding hairline.

I held her tightly, feeling the warmth of her body through the floral dress she was wearing. No matter what the time of day or the occasion, my mother always took great pride in her appearance. This applied even when she was doing housework or cooking, as she was right now. Her only concession was an apron, worn over a dress or a skirt. She was not interested in the growing preference of women for trousers or jeans.

I didn't want to let go and squeezed her even harder, closing my eyes and allowing memories of my childhood to flood through me. I had returned to a time when she was still the centrepiece of my universe. Yes, I might have been ten, and I was no cry-baby, but she was still the one I ran to for comfort when I needed to. This was often due to fights with friends, such as the day Martin Cooper had thrown a lump of brick at me and smashed my head open. Had that happened yet? It must have been around this time. I reached up to my forehead to run my fingers over the scar. It wasn't there.

Right now, it wasn't comfort from some childhood woe that I needed. This was just a natural reaction to the sheer joy of being with her again. I couldn't just feel her, I could smell her in the warm embrace; the faint aroma of her perfume mingling with the aroma of coffee, toast, and the fireplace filling me with a sense of security, familiarity, and belonging. Nothing in my adult world had ever come close to matching this, even when I thought I had been in love. I desperately wanted to prolong the moment but knew I could not hold on to her indefinitely.

"Sorry, Mum," I said, reluctantly breaking off the hug. To try to justify my unashamed burst of affection, I added, "I just had a horrible dream in which you flew to New York and the plane crashed and you died."

As I spoke, I looked down at the bracelet which was glowing green. I didn't have a clue what I was doing but it seemed to be the right thing. The plane crash, just like the incident that led to the lifelong scar on my forehead, hadn't happened yet.

"Oh, Nick, that's awful, but it was only a bad dream. You don't have to worry. I'm not planning on going to New York anytime soon or anywhere else on a plane, come to that. Chance would be a fine thing. The nearest I'm likely to get to going abroad is the Isle of Wight."

She was wrong, but she had no way of knowing that. 1981 was going to be the year she was going to get her big break. It was one she had yearned for ever since she had picked up a paintbrush as a young girl and begun her journey to becoming an incredibly talented artist. Inspired by the classic works of Thomas Gainsborough and John Constable, she had taken to bringing the world around us to life on canvas.

From the farmyard to beyond, her works had drawn praise from her schoolteachers at an early age. Now, she regularly showcased and sold her art at our annual village carnival. In addition, they adorned the walls not only of our cottage but also that of the farmhouse next door where she had grown up. There her parents, Jack, and Nellie Cartwright, still lived in 1981.

Apart from some local recognition, Mum had not been able to take her talent further thus far. She had grown up in an era where the practical requirements of the farm meant that going to any sort of art college wasn't considered. But she never lost heart and produced several pieces a year depicting the local area, both out on location and from her workshop at the side of the house. Then, in 1981, her big moment came. She was finally discovered by the art world. And that big break had killed her.

These events might have been long in the past for me but I had never got over them. Who would? Yet suddenly, here I was and they were no longer set in stone. Looking up at her I resolved that whatever else this year had in store, there was one thing I would be prioritising over all others.

She was exactly as I remembered her, preserved forever as if she had been frozen in time in her final days. Her jet-black hair, always completely straight, stopped just above her shoulders and was just beginning to show hints of grey now she was in her early forties. Her face was warm, with clear blue eyes, with just a hint of weathering beginning to show. Her face, even now in the middle of winter, still had plenty of colour thanks to a life in which she had spent plenty of time outdoors.

When she wasn't painting or looking after our home, she still worked on the farm as much as she could.

The most striking thing about her was that she seemed so big and I don't mean in a plus size way. It was because I was barely five feet tall at the age of ten. I could see I was going to have to adjust to a world where I was small again. People forget as they get older how much bigger the world seemed when you were small. It only becomes noticeable when you revisit a childhood place as an adult. My assembly hall at primary school seemed like a vast cathedral when I was little but when I went back as an adult for a charity event, years later, I couldn't believe how tiny it was. I wondered how I would perceive it now. I would soon find out because, in a few days, I would be going back to school.

Once I had recovered from my initial euphoria at seeing Mum again, I took some time to look around the room. I had smelt the toast when I came down and looked across to the cooker where she was preparing breakfast. This was proper homemade bread that she baked herself, another tradition from our farming background.

She didn't use a toaster as our old-fashioned stove was equipped with an overhead grill. Slices of bread could be watched at eye level and turned over once one side was done. I wondered why this design had gone out of fashion as I hadn't seen one in years. Toasters were convenient but not always practical. You couldn't do cheese on toast in them for a start. Not without making an awful mess.

The cottages in the lane were built in the early nineteenth century when land space didn't command the premium that it did in the modern world. This meant they were well spaced out in addition to being generously spacious inside. There was plenty of room in our kitchen for a large pine table in the centre of the room that could comfortably seat six, and we had a separate dining room too. The kitchen was full of period features such as wooden beams and an open fireplace, one of two in the house. This one had originally been used for cooking but since modern ovens had arrived, it was used just for heating.

Our house was the largest of the five cottages in the lane, boasting three decent bedrooms upstairs and a full-sized bathroom. This had also once been a bedroom but had been converted some years ago. The outside toilet, which had previously been the only available facility, was still present in a small outbuilding at the bottom of the garden. Thankfully it was no longer in use, the building being used only for storage by the 1980s and as a home for the local spiders.

Not all the cottages had been modernised. I recalled that old Stan and Edna further down the lane still didn't have a proper bathroom when I was a kid because I had seen him making his way down his garden in the morning with a copy of the *Daily Mirror* under his arm. I wasn't sure if he was reading it or wiping his bottom on it.

Almost everything was homemade in our house, including the butter which came from the farm, and the marmalade which my mother was now lovingly spreading on my toast. I had forgotten how great it was having everything done for me. Kids never realise how lucky they are until the harsh reality of adult life kicks in and they must fend for themselves.

There are a lot of things that are different when you are a kid that you forget about later. One of the first things I noticed was how lithe and full of energy I was when I got out of bed. I felt so light it was as if I was walking on the moon. And there was not an ache, pain, or blemish in sight. That's probably why when people are young they don't understand why all the old gits are always going on about being tired or their ailments. By old git, I mean anyone over thirty-five, which seems positively ancient when you are ten.

"Are you looking forward to the party tonight?" asked Mum, shaking me out of these random patterns of thought.

Of course, the party. It was New Year's Day which meant the family tribe would be descending upon us for the last leg of the Christmas circuit which took place every year. Between Christmas Eve and today, there were no fewer than five such gatherings. The rota was set in stone and I could not recall any deviation from it while I was growing up in the 1970s. But this would be the final year. By the end of 1981, the family would have been torn apart to an extent where things could never be the same again.

With plenty to prepare, Mum was already up to her elbows in the kitchen, despite it being only around half past eight. She was busy kneading some pastry which I guessed would be for making sausage rolls, one of her specialities. The idea of purchasing such items from a supermarket would have been sacrilege at this time, besides which, in the village, we did not have one.

Other than a small Spar and a Londis, all our shops were traditional independents from butchers to greengrocers. We even had an old-fashioned ironmongery. These were long gone by 2020, put out of business in the 1990s after a large Sainsbury was built on a new industrial estate on the outskirts of the village, along with a Homebase and drive-thru Burger King. Although I disapproved, it was somewhat hypocritical for me to do so, given that I worked for one of the largest food chains in the country. Companies like mine had been crushing small businesses for decades by then.

Now I was back in the past, I couldn't help thinking how much we had lost as a society, letting so much of that old world disappear. I was looking forward to spending time while I was here visiting all these old shops. It would help me answer a question I had been pondering. Were the old days better, or did we have an exaggerated nostalgic view of them? I would have plenty of time to find out.

"Where's Dad?" I asked, in two minds about how I felt about seeing him again. Unlike Mum, whose persona was preserved as I had last seen her, he would not be the same mellowed man I had last spoken to on the phone on Christmas Day, less than a week before he died. This was the younger version; the one that this year would get involved with Tracy. It was still hard to get the thought of that out of my head. How could he have done it?

"He's still in bed," replied Mum. "He had a bit of a skinful last night and he's sleeping it off."

That wasn't surprising. On New Year's Eve we always gathered at Uncle William's house, three doors down, where he liked to show off his year's crop of homemade wines. These were made from various dubious-sounding ingredients, from dandelions to nettles, yet he swore they were the best wines you could lay your hands on this side of Bordeaux. Reactions from the assembled family were mixed at best, but however they tasted, they did what they said on the tin. I had grown used to spending these end-of-year gatherings watching my various aunts and uncles drunkenly see in the New Year.

I was too young to be allowed to indulge but there was always Coca-Cola or Corona lemonade on offer at William's, rare treats in those leaner times. Fizzy drinks still had a treat status about them back then. They were bought only for parties and Christmas, while we made do with cheap orange squash packed with E numbers the rest of the time.

I was reluctant to leave Mum, feeling a desire to throw a protective ring around her, but I needed to approach this sensibly. She was in no immediate danger. The plane crash that would take her life wasn't until the summer. I had plenty of time to consider what to do about that. So, still in my standard issue Marks & Spencer navy pyjamas, I took myself off to my bedroom to get dressed.

Alone in my room, I donned an impossibly small pair of jeans and a stripy blue and red sweatshirt. Then I had a good look around, having leapt out of bed and torn straight down the stairs when I had first woken up. I felt as if I was exploring an exhibit in a museum dedicated to my life. I wanted to look at everything all at the same time and it was overwhelming. So many memories. Where to start?

Scattered around on the floor were several *Star Wars* figures. These toys had been huge when I was a kid. All my friends collected them, from the individual figures which were around four inches tall, right up to the gold standard of the range – the Millennium Falcon. Only James Spencer, who lived in one of the big houses on Church Lane, had one of those. I had plenty of the smaller toys though, particularly the action figures who were within the reach of my pocket money at 99p a pop.

My favourite was Darth Vader who could extend a small piece of coloured plastic out of the end of his arm to represent a lightsabre. I picked him up from the floor and staged a quick mock battle with Luke Skywalker, who I noted was missing half an arm. Then I remembered I had cut it off in tribute to a scene in the latest film. Perhaps I shouldn't have done that. In hindsight, I shouldn't have played with these toys at all. I should have kept them pristine in their boxes. But how was I to know, at such a tender age, that these toys would one day become prized collectors' items, some changing hands for thousands of pounds?

It was a shame my wallpaper did not match the toys. My room had a space-age feel to it, thanks to the scenes of spaceships and planets all over the wall but they were nothing to do with *Star Wars*. I knew you could get *Star Wars* wallpaper because James had that too. James had everything. I had seen it at one of his birthday parties and begged my parents for the same for my ninth birthday. They seemed receptive to the idea but where they went wrong was asking my Uncle Dennis, a painter and decorator by trade, to buy it and put it up as a birthday present.

Unfortunately, Dennis made the mistake of taking Aunt Edith to the shop to buy the wallpaper and when she saw the cost per roll, she baulked at the price. Then she spotted some similar wallpaper, to her untrained eye, in a bargain bin being practically given away for 50p a roll. Being Aunt Edith, she naturally talked Dennis into buying this, and so it was, after being taken for a day out to Cotswold Wildlife Park, I came home to find this stuff all over the walls.

The offending paper was from a movie called *The Black Hole*, which I had never heard of. I later found out it was one of several inferior copycat movies that had been hastily made in the late 1970s in a doomed attempt to replicate the success of *Star Wars*.

"This is just as good," I remember Aunt Edith insisting at the time, which it most certainly was not. When I reacted in a lukewarm manner I was told I was an ungrateful little sod and sent to bed early, not for the first time. Dennis, who I didn't care for, was also angry and threatened to give me a clip around the ear. Children were expected to be seen and not heard in our family, as Edith never tired of saying. Opinions that contradicted those of the adults were swiftly dealt with, even if the adults were wrong. Which in this case, they most certainly were.

I could have bought a *Star Wars* figure every week with my pocket money, presented to me each Saturday. That crisp green pound note felt like a fortune when I was a kid. Paper money always felt more valuable than coins and I didn't like it when the note was abolished. The amount of pocket money my friends got varied enormously and it seemed that a pound was quite generous for the time. Unless you were James from Church Lane, of course. That spoilt little shit got a fiver.

Some spent their money on toys, some on sweets, while others frittered it away on football stickers. What a waste of money they were. Anyone who has ever attempted to complete one of these albums must have realised after a certain point what a fruitless endeavour it was. I learnt this the hard way with my *Football '80* album, which I could see right now on the bookshelf, still unfinished. The manufacturers claimed that they printed the stickers in even numbers but I had a keen eye for probability, being something of a maths prodigy. How could it be statistically valid that I had about twenty Peter Shiltons and no Glenn Hoddles? And that wasn't just down to random bad luck. No one in the entire school had Glen Hoddle.

The thing I most liked to spend my money on was records, specifically 7" singles. I had begged for my own record player for my tenth birthday, and unlike the wallpaper disaster of the previous year, this time my prayers were answered. My parents got hold of a second-hand one from the classified ads in the local paper and although it was far from being in mint condition, it did what I needed it to do.

Harman's ironmongery in the village, for some bizarre but welcome reason, stocked the latest chart singles, meaning there was no need to travel to Oxford to get them. At 79p, they were well within my remit and I tended to buy about two a month. So by now, five months after my birthday I had twelve, plus a couple of albums which I had received for Christmas. Leaving

Darth Vader and Luke on the floor, I began sifting through my collection now.

Everyone, at least before the age of streaming, remembers buying their first single. In my case, it was the novelty track, 'Two Pints of Lager and a Packet of Crisps Please' by the oddly named Splodgenessabounds. It was probably not the coolest track ever but I like to think it holds a certain niche value in the quirkiness that is British pop history. Later, it even had a sitcom named after it. But it was the single I bought the following week that I was most keen to play. This was the one I should have bought first.

I slipped the vinyl from the cover, placed it on the turntable, and pressed the plastic button that would set off the mechanism to automatically place the needle on the record. Then, a second or two later, Joy Division's 'Love Will Tear Us Apart' began playing from the two small speakers that had come with the player. It was admittedly tinny, being only a very basic model, but that hadn't mattered at the time and it didn't matter now. It still sounded loud in the confines of my room so I turned the volume down, not wanting to get a telling-off from Dad who was still in bed. Then I looked through the others, rediscovering long-lost gems from The Undertones, Split Enz and others.

To my regret, in 2020 I no longer had these singles. I had given them away to a charity shop in 2005 when CDs and then downloads had rendered vinyl seemingly obsolete. I hadn't wanted to do it but I was getting divorced, had to move house, and was cleaning out my old life. What a mistake that had been. Perhaps I could do something about it. What if I were to get some stickers, write a message on them telling me not to give them away, and then slap them on the covers? As this thought went through my head, the jewel on the bracelet on my wrist glowed green. It looked like this was a good idea, then.

I could have stayed in my room all day but I was keen to get out and explore the neighbourhood. I knew it inside out already so by explore I guess I meant revisit places long gone and compare them with their modern equivalent. The abandoned old mill was one place that sprang to mind. It was a fascinating, not to mention dangerous, place to play as kids but by 2020 it was gone, replaced by a petrol station on a bypass which didn't exist in 1981.

When I returned at lunchtime from my first walk around the village, I had my first encounter with my father and my sister as the four of us sat down to lunch together. This was just a light sandwich with a bit of salad. With the mountain of food that was being prepared for the family gathering in the evening, this was more than sufficient.

As we ate, it struck me that this might be one of the last times the four of us would eat together as a family. I looked across at Linda, to whom I had once been so close. Sadly, this year would be the year I would lose her. In truth, I probably already had.

There was a big age gap between us, almost nine years, which was a problem. Nine years might not sound much, but the gulf between me at ten and her at nineteen had become insurmountable. We were a generation apart when it came to music and culture and it made me determined if I ever had kids to have them close together. But I never got that chance.

We began to drift apart in September 1980 when she went away to study chemistry at Cambridge. Before that, she had spent her whole life in Meadowbrook Lane around the cottages and the farm, but once she discovered a new life elsewhere, her attitude to her roots changed.

We didn't see her for three months, and when she returned for Christmas, she was radically different. From the rural country girl she had been before, all skirts, jumpers and pigtails, she had morphed into a sophisticated political animal, full of opinions on anything and everything. She was also extremely condescending about all aspects of her heritage.

Her physical appearance had changed too, with dungarees now her preferred outfit, and her previously long dark hair, formerly like my mother's, now bleached and tightly cropped to barely an inch in length. She had acquired studs in both her ears as well as her nose. It was as if a different person had come home from the one we sent off in September, rather like when television producers change the actor in a soap opera. After this Christmas, other than a brief return for my mother's funeral, she would never come back again.

As for Dad, he was in his prime, lean and fit thanks to his job as a self-employed carpenter. He was good with his hands and when he wasn't working was frequently fixing some problem at home, on the farm, or in one of the other cottages.

"Hello, Nick," he said. "Where were you this morning? I thought you were going to help me with the logs."

"Logs?" I asked, wondering what he was on about.

"Yes, don't you remember our chat last night about you wanting more pocket money so you can buy more records? I said it was fine provided you worked for it. And we agreed you would take over the job of chopping the logs for here and the farmhouse to save me a job."

"Sorry, I must have forgotten, and besides, you were still in bed when I went out," I ventured. Of course I had forgotten. It was forty years ago. How could I be expected to remember?

"That's not a problem because we can still do it this afternoon. I'll show you the correct way to handle an axe."

"I don't think we should be burning wood at all," said Linda, before launching into a monologue about the environment and the rainforests. I didn't necessarily disagree with anything she was saying but I recalled that we had been treated to a barrage of these preachy little speeches since she had returned from university.

"Whatever you say, dear," said Mum condescendingly, generating a look of fury from Linda. Her reaction filled me with glee. Good old Mum, letting her rant on, and then dismissing the whole thing with four words rather than being drawn into an argument. I had so much more in common with her than I did with Dad. In some of my darker moments over the years, the thought had come to me that it was the wrong parent that had died. I know it's wrong to think that way but I'm guessing I'm not the only one ever to have such thoughts. Not wanting to hear any more of it, I decided to chip in and change the subject.

"Anyway, Dad, how's your head this morning? Did the lie-in help?"

He chuckled. "Oh, I've been worse. William's concoctions certainly pack a punch. I was taking it easy last night."

Linda rolled her eyes. "You say that every year, Dad. This family is so predictable."

I said little more over lunch, not wanting to put my foot in it. I was still finding my way and didn't want to say anything that might seem odd while I was getting to grips with things. What I didn't have any trouble getting the hang of was the chopping of the logs, with which Dad was seriously impressed. And so he should have been, after all I had learned how to do this already, forty years before. If it earned me a little cash, all the better. I might need it later.

It was cold in the farmyard where the chopping block was located, and I was glad to get back into the warmth of the kitchen as dusk approached. The guests would be arriving soon. Edith was already there, fussing over the food my mother had prepared earlier. She was thirteen years older than Mum and this often showed in their conversations when Edith sometimes sounded like she was talking to a child rather than a younger sibling.

"No, no, Mary, this won't do. You've made far too many sausage rolls. How many are we expecting this evening?"

"About eighteen, by my reckoning. There's Mum and Dad, the four of us and the four of you for starters. William, Jackie, Tracy, Henry, and Carol. Oh, and I've invited the Fosters too."

"Invited themselves, no doubt. Anywhere there's any free food going. I notice they never invite us to their place. Twenty years since they bought Sunflower after Uncle George passed on, and I've not seen inside it since. You shouldn't have told her about it."

"You know what Brenda's like," replied my mother. "You can't organise anything around here without her finding out. Besides, we do it every year. She's figured out the routine."

"Don't I know it? I sometimes think that nose of hers is glued to that window. Anyway, you've got twenty-four sausage rolls here. You don't need to make that many. One per person at most, and even then that's probably too much because not everybody likes them. Waste not, want not. Also, I notice you've used an awful lot of sausage meat. I wouldn't have put that much in. Oh, hello, Nick," she added, noticing my presence for the first time.

"Hello, Aunt Edith," I said, looking at her rake-thin figure and thinking she wouldn't have put any meat in at all if she could have got away with it. I was going to have to be very careful with my tongue. It would be so easy to say something sarcastic or scathing but too much of that and I'd find myself facing an early night, and I couldn't have that. I was looking forward to making the most of the opportunity to get reacquainted with the family this evening.

"And what are you up to, young man? Helping your mother, I hope?"

"I was helping Dad, actually," I said. "Chopping logs. It was thirsty work, though. Can I have a drink?"

"There's some fizzy pop in the dining room," said Mum. "It's for tonight, but I guess no one's going to miss a drop."

"You shouldn't be buying them pop, Mary," scolded Edith. "It's overpriced rubbish and it rots the teeth. Water's always been good enough for my two. It's all they had in the Garden of Eden. Adam's Ale, they called it. That was what the Lord provided and it was good enough for them."

"Why did Jesus turn it into wine, then?" I asked. I had forgotten that Edith was religious.

"Don't ask impudent questions, child," replied Edith. "Mary, you really need to teach this boy more respect."

"OK, I'll just have some water," I said, grabbing a plastic beaker from the side and sticking it under the tap. It didn't pay to anger Edith, or her husband Dennis, come to that.

Over the next hour or so, our guests arrived, greeting each other as if they hadn't seen each other for years, which was ridiculous. They had already spent Christmas Eve, Christmas Day, Boxing Day, and New Year's Eve together. You would have thought they would have been sick of the sight of each other by now. In some ways it was touching, having the whole family together again. But in other ways it was excruciating.

Take Auntie Carol and Uncle Henry, for example. Carol was the second oldest of the four siblings and the only one who did not live in Meadowbrook Lane. The two of them lived in a posh house in Boars Hill, a few miles away, and were comfortably better off than the rest of us. This was something that Carol never missed an opportunity to slip into the conversation. The wealth wasn't of her making. It was all down to Henry who had done very well for himself in the property business, though the precise nature of what he did was never discussed.

I didn't dislike Carol particularly – the best adjective I can think to describe her is jolly. She was plump and extravagant, much to the ire of frugal Edith, and unsurprisingly, the two of them did not get on. She was a lot friendlier than Edith but that came with some notable disadvantages.

Firstly, she insisted on giving me a huge, sloppy kiss every time she saw me, right up until the age of about sixteen. By then it was becoming seriously inappropriate. And when I say sloppy, I'm not exaggerating. The woman was always caked in make-up, including bright red lipstick that never failed to leave an imprint on my cheek or wherever else she decided to plant one, including the lips which she didn't consider off limits.

Secondly, there was the perfume that went with it. Unlike my mother, who only wore a light touch of cologne, Carol reeked of whatever scent it was she coated herself in every time she went out. Sometimes I wondered if she bathed in it. The compulsory hug and kiss transferred enough of this stuff onto me to ensure that I would go around for the rest of the day smelling like a tart's boudoir. Strangely, my cousin Simon was spared this routine. Perhaps it was because he was Edith's son rather than Mary's.

Another annoying thing about Carol was that these encounters always began the same way, with the same predictable phrases that she parroted. It was rather like a Dalek toy I had upstairs. It had a string I could pull, that would prompt it to emit one of about half a dozen stock phrases. Carol's conversation was similarly limited.

I braced myself for what was to come as she walked through the front door, laden in make-up and wearing a lavish mink fur coat which would have had her lynched if she wore it in the future that I had come from. Linda had already given her a ton of stick about it the previous night but it hadn't deterred her from wearing it again.

"Ooh, haven't you grown," she gushed which was a ridiculous statement, considering she had only seen me the previous evening. This was stock phrase number one and it was followed swiftly by number two.

"Come here and give Auntie a kiss," she demanded. I didn't see that I had any choice but to comply so I screwed up my eyes and waited for the inevitable lipstick and perfume assault on my face. Meanwhile Henry strode past, pipe in mouth, heading no doubt for the scotch on the sideboard in the lounge. I noticed he hadn't brought any with him, and there was me thinking Edith was the tight one.

After my mother, the two people I had been looking forward to seeing most were my grandparents, Jack and Nellie Cartwright. They were very much still the head of the clan, despite now being in their eighties. When I was growing up, I spent as much time at the farmhouse as I did at home. I don't know if it was because they were older and more mellow but they just seemed genuinely more approachable, less stressed, and more welcoming than most of the generation below.

Jack, remarkably, had lived in the farmhouse his entire life, other than when he was away fighting in the First World War. One of three brothers, he was the only one to come home alive and it was in the early 1920s that he reconnected with his childhood sweetheart, the daughter of the local blacksmith.

They were married in 1924 and Edith came along just a year later. After they passed on, I wished I had asked them more about their lives. Now, when they walked in, still sprightly, I realised I now had the chance. But it wouldn't be tonight. I wasn't going to get the chance to reacquaint myself fully with anyone tonight. There were just too many people coming back into my life in too short a time. There was no rush; I had the whole year.

Dennis arrived, in the same scruffy clothes he wore to work, along with my cousins Julia and Simon. They were swiftly followed by a younger Brenda, with her husband, Robert, and clone daughter, Karen. Last to arrive were William, Jackie, and the one person I was in two minds about seeing, the dreaded Tracy.

Here she was, the seventeen-year-old temptress who was to wreak such devastation on my life in the future. Up until now, I had thought that it was only after my Mum's death that she got her claws into Dad but looking at her now as she walked through the door I had cause to question that.

Her outrageously provocative outfit couldn't have looked more out of place next to the other conservatively dressed inhabitants of Meadowbrook Lane, apart from my sister. She wore a short black leather jacket over a white low-cut blouse which flirted shamelessly with the boundaries of decency, revealing an almost obscene amount of cleavage. Together with the daring short black leather skirt, above a pair of fishnet stockings and red high heels, she looked like she was dressing to attract someone's eye – but whose? As if I couldn't guess.

She was even outdoing Carol on the make-up front, her green eyes framed by dark eyeshadow, and lips caked in rich red gloss. This, along with her spiky dark hair, gave her a gothic look which put me in mind of the singer out of Siouxsie and the Banshees.

Tracy was clearly confident in her appearance because of the way she held herself. She walked confidently, almost brazenly, with her head held high, clearly not giving a toss about what anyone might think or say about her appearance. I was pretty sure some there would have something to say, especially Edith and Brenda, but whether it would be to her face or not was another matter.

"Wotcha, Nick," she said, as she passed me into the house. "How's it hanging?"

I don't think she expected a response as she walked straight past me into the living room, probably in search of some booze. She was almost eighteen, and with the drinking culture that pervaded our family, no one was likely to disapprove, except possibly Edith. She didn't approve of anything.

Her look had set my mind working overtime. Did she already have designs on my father at this stage? I decided that I would watch the two of them like a hawk and find out, a thought that interestingly elicited a green pulse from the bracelet. Perhaps I was onto something.

Everyone had gathered in the living room for drinks and I made my way through to join them. Although it was a spacious cottage, there were limits, and it felt crowded with eighteen or so people packed into one room. There was a steady hubbub of noise as the conversations flowed. They didn't seem to have run out of things to talk about, even after the extended period of festive gatherings.

There was a stereo system in the lounge that was much better than mine but if I was hoping for a 1980s music nostalgia fest, I was to be disappointed. My father had chosen music from his generation, so it was Buddy Holly and Bill Haley who were providing the soundtrack to the evening.

As was often the case, the wives had gathered on the large red three-piece suite, while the men stayed close to the drinks tray.

"Oh, I do love your new carpet, Mary," said Carol, which came, like most things she said, with a noticeable condescending touch. The unspoken words that you could almost hear her thinking were *but it's not as good as ours*.

"Yes, I got it from that new place in Witney," she replied. "Now that the children are older I thought it was safe to get a new one."

I looked down at the deep pile carpet which was plush and a light cream colour. Then I glanced across to the men by the sideboard to check out the red wine stain on the carpet roughly the same shape as Africa. No matter what Mum had tried to get it out, it had never completely disappeared, continuing to be visible many years after her death. But like the scar on my head, it wasn't there yet.

"Ah, yes, not a bad drop of scotch that," said Henry, who was alternating between sips from his crystal glass and puffs on his pipe as he held court at the sideboard with Dennis and Dad. "Obviously, it's not up to the quality of the malt we had at my place the other day, but beggars can't be choosers, eh?"

"You didn't think to bring a bottle along, then?" asked Dennis, who looked rather forlorn in his hole-ridden cardigan, standing next to Henry in his suit and waistcoat. Dennis always looked scruffy and had acquired the nickname 'Worzel' from some of the other kids in the neighbourhood. Edith didn't believe in buying new clothes. 'Make do and mend' was one of her many mottos but this green, bedraggled garment, covered in paint stains, should have been put out of its misery years ago.

"You know it's the funniest thing, I said to Carol, we must take a bottle along, and it was only when we got here, that I realised I'd left it in the drawing room."

"Yes, that seems to happen a lot," remarked Dennis, drily. "Most recently last night, I recall. I could have done with a drop of malt then to get rid of the taste of that dreadful turnip wine William forced on us."

"Edith seemed to enjoy it," said Dad.

"Of course she did, it was free," replied Dennis. He had lived with her penny-pinching ways for so many years he was more than happy to joke about it with the others when she was out of earshot.

I watched as Tracy approached the three of them, making a beeline for Dad.

"Excuse me, Uncle Tony, could you fix me a drink?" she said, flashing her eyes coyly at him. I was left in no doubt as to her intentions, but he, to his credit, gave no sign of responding. So perhaps it hadn't started yet, even though she was giving him all the right signals. Or maybe he was just hiding it well. I suppose it was natural for me to blame her but it takes two to tango.

"What are you having?"

"Vodka and orange, if that's OK?"

"I don't see why not," said Dad, reaching for the Smirnoff. "The orange is in the fridge." Casting his eye around, he alighted on me, and added, "Nick, go and get the orange juice from the fridge for Tracy, would you?"

Great, now I was running errands for the pair of them. Complying, I headed out to the kitchen where I was taken aback to see Brenda rummaging around in one of the kitchen drawers.

"Oh, Nick," she said, taken aback. "I was just looking for a butter knife…"

"Of course you were," I said sarcastically. I was tired of biting my tongue and it was only Brenda. She wasn't even family and held no power over me. "That isn't the drawer we keep the cutlery in, that's where my parents keep their bills and other paperwork."

"There's no need to take that tone with me, young man. I've got a good mind to have a word with your parents."

"Go ahead. I'm sure they'll be interested to know why you were nosing about in their private affairs. Besides, there are a pile of butter knives on the dining room table. Didn't you see them?"

"Did I say butter knife? I meant tea towel."

"Two things that are easily confused," I continued, keeping up the sarcastic tone. "There's a big pile of them on the counter, just in front of you."

"So there is," she said, as I walked over to the fridge to fetch the orange juice, having rather enjoyed our little exchange as she scuttled off back to the living room.

After I had taken Tracy her orange juice, I was unable to continue my surveillance of her and my father as I was accosted by my cousin Simon. He was just over a year older than me and had gone up to big school in the summer. He was most insistent that we go upstairs for a game of Battleships which quite appealed as I hadn't played the game for years. So we went up to my room for a while until we were summoned downstairs to eat.

The table in the dining room was groaning under the weight of the food. The farm was much smaller than it had been when Jack was born but still generated plenty of produce and we always ate well at these functions, usually a cold buffet. As I piled my plate high with sausage rolls I was scolded by Edith, who was monitoring the area to ensure no one took more than their fair share.

"Don't be greedy, Nick! One per person, remember. And why do you need all that bread?"

It was only two slices, but I suppose she had a point. I loved my food but was going to have to adjust my calorie intake to child-size portions. I didn't intend to spend 1981 turning my younger self into a bloater. What was most frustrating was that I couldn't have any alcohol. I could have just fancied some of that scotch. That was the cry of a fifty-year-old mind in a ten-year-old body still adapting to the change.

And that was just an internal struggle. Dealing with other people was far more problematic. In every interaction I had throughout that evening, it was clear that I was expected to conform to the hierarchy. I was the kid and they were the adults so my opinion was worthless. And of the kids present I was the youngest, which meant that I was at the bottom of the pecking order among my cousins too. But I did, in the end, manage to do something to draw some rare praise. What's more, it gave me my first experience of how to use the bracelet.

During the drunken cringe-fest that was the compulsory game of charades, the bracelet began pulsing red on my arm. And then a thought popped into my head, seemingly from nowhere. It related to something that had crossed my mind during Carol and my mother's conversation about the carpet earlier. Now, I was convinced that this was the night on which it had been ruined, and what's more I suddenly remembered with complete clarity exactly how and when it was going to happen. It was as if the bracelet had reached into my mind, and plucked out the memory, in preparation for what was to come.

I recalled that Simon had sneaked himself some of the untouched wine that William had brought along when no one was looking. As he was only eleven, it had a rather adverse effect on him. During the charades, he suddenly jumped up and shouted, "Guess who I am!" waving his arms around crazily at the same time.

"Magnus Pyke," called out his sister Julia. She was ten years older than him and worked as a hairdresser at a salon in the village. It was a trait in our family to leave big age gaps between the siblings. Anyway, she was correct in her guess. Pyke was a television scientist of the period who was rather enthusiastic with his arm gestures. And so it was that Simon knocked an almost full bottle of red wine that had just been uncorked onto the floor, to the horror of everyone assembled as they watched its contents ooze across the brand-new carpet.

That was how it had happened before. But not today because the moment had been prepared for. Racing across the room at the precise time, I dived to catch the bottle in a manoeuvre which Ian Botham would have been proud of. Other than a few drops that escaped and landed on my jeans, I kept the bottle upright and the carpet remained intact.

"Howzat?" I exclaimed and for a few minutes, I wasn't the annoying little kid, I was the hero. And Simon got a bollocking too, so that was a bonus. I'm not sure what the cousin equivalent of sibling rivalry is called but whatever it is, this was one occasion where I had come out on top.

The evening wore on, the family grew steadily merrier, and eventually I felt tired and went to bed. I was pleased that I had performed my first good deed but I still had much to learn. As had been amply demonstrated, my youth meant I had little power or say in things at home, and no doubt at school it would be the same. It was difficult to see how I was going to be able to emulate the sort of things Keith had managed to do when he had gone back in time. Thankfully, a nuclear attack on Meadowbrook Lane seemed an unlikely prospect.

But it was only day one and the year was young. I had saved the carpet but I was sure I hadn't been sent back in time just for that. There would be plenty more to do but no matter what came my way, all of it paled into insignificance against what had to be the number one reason I had come back to 1981.

I was here to save Mum's life and until that was achieved, absolutely nothing else mattered.

February 1981

By the time the calendar ticked over into February, I had successfully adapted back into my childhood persona.

It hadn't been easy to begin with. Each day brought challenges, casting me into situations I had long forgotten how to deal with. But once thrown in the deep end it was amazing how quickly I adapted. It was as if my brain was a vast archive of hundreds of dusty filing cabinets, tucked away in a vault underground, untouched for decades. Then, when the drawers were opened, the contents were retrieved from their long hibernation. In many cases the bracelet helped too, pulsing green or red to guide me, and sometimes I was convinced it was putting thoughts directly into my head.

I spent a lot of time wandering around the village in a wistful frame of mind, comparing snapshots of the past with my knowledge of the future. I also got reacquainted with friends, most of whom I had long lost touch with. That was the thing about growing up in the 1980s. There was no permanent link to people like there is in the twenty-first century via email and social media.

Of course, back in the twentieth century people did make the effort to stay in touch via letters and phone calls but that's the whole point. It requires a degree of effort to handwrite a letter, put it in an envelope, stick a stamp on it, and take it to a post box. It's all too much like hard work for many people, especially once life takes them all in different directions.

During school holidays and weekends there was a small group of boys that I hung out with, one of whom was Simon. We didn't get on particularly well and probably wouldn't have been friends if we were not cousins both living in Meadowbrook Lane. Two other kids formed the core membership of our little gang. Philip and Martin both lived on one of the new council estates a few streets away, and were in the same year as me at the local primary school.

Philip was quite easy-going and tried to avoid conflict, but Martin had a fearsome reputation for being the hardest kid in school. He thought nothing of giving a good hiding to another boy he took a dislike to. I should know, it had happened to me enough times. Strangely, few consequences ever seemed to come from his thuggery, even if it happened at school. The prevailing attitude from grown-ups in those days was that it was just boys being boys.

I don't know if things have changed since my time because I don't have kids of my own, but my impression is that schools and parents are a lot tougher now on any behaviour that could be construed as bullying. The thing about Martin was that it wasn't a sustained or planned campaign of bullying. We were friends most of the time but then there was a moment of hot-headedness which would lead to a kick or a punch over some flashpoint. This used to happen a lot.

Frequently, the four of us would be playing out and things would descend into an argument. It would either be two against two or three against one. But Martin was never the one facing off against the other three because Simon always took his side, the coward. First there would be name-calling, then a little rough and tumble which might just be some pushing and shoving.

Sometimes it would end there but more frequently it would develop into kicking and punching. And that wasn't all.

On several occasions, things would escalate to the point where projectiles were brought into use. By that, I mean we thought nothing of picking up stones, bits of broken glass, sticks, or anything else that was to hand and throwing them at each other. It was only now I was experiencing it again first-hand that I realised how violent it all was. We were a bunch of little hooligans, particularly Martin. Once our battles were over we would all go home and it would be swiftly forgotten. By the next day, we'd meet up to play as normal and all would be well until the next time it happened.

Eventually, and probably inevitably, it led to a serious incident. I knew that, at some future flashpoint, I was going to get a huge gash above the eye from a half brick lobbed in my direction. It was only then, after I needed hospital treatment, that our parents cottoned on to what was going on and gave us all a strict lecture.

The sticks and stones stopped after that but the occasional thump here and there was still an occupational hazard of being friends with Martin. It did have an upside too. When he was on my side, which he was most of the time, I didn't have to worry about hassle from any other kids. No one gave Martin any crap – they didn't dare.

Obviously, getting my head split open was something I hoped to avoid so I tried to will the bracelet to warn me when the time came. I still wasn't sure if I could transmit my thoughts to it in this way but it was worth a try.

The day of the brick-throwing event arrived on the first weekend of February when we ventured down to the crumbling relic which had formerly been a mill on a tributary feeding the Thames. This forsaken structure had been abandoned for decades, since at least the 1930s according to my grandparents, and it showed. We had been warned not to go near it under any circumstances as the building wasn't considered to be safe.

Being kids, that was like a red rag to a bull to us. Dangerous equalled fun in our eyes, and the mill was far from the only dodgy place we got into. The world I grew up in was littered with these old, decaying buildings but after the property boom got going properly in the late 1980s they all disappeared. The land they were on was too valuable to go to waste. Until then, they were left to rot.

Technically we were trespassing, not that anyone seemed to care, and it wasn't as if we were breaking in. Almost nothing was left of the door thanks to a combination of decay and previous generations of errant youths who had ripped apart what was left of the rotting wood to gain access.

Inside, the air always seemed heavy and damp, even in the summer. At this time of year it was exceptionally grim, giving it an almost haunted feel. It was completely exposed to the elements, with several parts of the roof gone. With the wet winter the country was currently experiencing, there were puddles on the stone floor which was covered with beer cans, broken bottles, and all the other crap that invariably litters these places.

Nature, relentless in its reclamation, was already taking hold with ivy staking a claim to the interior walls.

On one side, a tree branch was making good inroads through a shattered window. There was also graffiti everywhere, predominantly the anarchy symbol, a capital A in a circle, which seemed to be the most popular thing to spray on walls when I was growing up. Finally, there was a stained, abandoned mattress to complete the sordid picture, next to which I was disgusted to spot an empty Durex wrapper. Who the hell would be desperate enough to want to have sex in here?

The others didn't seem to notice the condom wrapper, and why would they? They probably didn't even know what it was. Sex education in the 1980s was minimal, and I have to say, I am not sure if at the age of ten, I had even known what a condom was. Certainly, in the month or so I had spent playing with Martin and the others, the topic of sex had not been mentioned.

I didn't know what possessed us to want to come here, it was horrible. I guess being somewhere that was out of bounds was reason enough but I didn't want to linger. I remembered now that it was here where I had been hit by the brick. It was when Martin began kicking at a crumbling brick wall with the toe of his Doc Martens, for no other reason besides the joy of mindless vandalism, that the bracelet began glowing red and I knew it was time to get out.

He dressed like what used to be called a bovver boy, in jeans and a white T-shirt, though today the effect was diluted by the presence of his blue Parka coat. We were all wearing them because our mothers insisted we did not go out without them at this time of year. His Doc Martens were an integral part of his outfit and he boasted that they had steel toecaps, which were coming in handy as he booted away at the decaying brickwork. To complete the look, he had short, cropped ginger hair, not yet short enough to be classed as a skinhead although years later that was the look he would adopt.

The wall he was vandalising ran across the centre of the structure, dividing the two main rooms. It had been in a sorry state for some time. On one of our previous visits, Martin had noticed some of the bricks were loose and kicked them out, creating a small hole which he promptly declared was now the toilet. He then took great pleasure in urinating through it. I know this sounds incredibly juvenile but the thing is, we were ten, and I must confess we all lined up to take a slash.

When he got bored with kicking the wall, Martin picked up an old piece of lead piping which he had wrenched off the wall on a previous visit. Using this, he began to try to prise away some of the more stubborn bricks, hell-bent on doing as much damage as he could. I'm not sure why he enjoyed wrecking things so much, perhaps he had a bad home life. I knew his dad wasn't around. Martin told us he was away on the oil rigs but my dad said that was a cover story for him being in prison.

Previously, I had no idea how much danger his actions were putting us in. I did now, though, and so did Philip because his dad was a builder and he was already helping him out in the family business. Normally, he was unquestioning of Martin, having wisely concluded it wasn't a good idea, but on this occasion he spoke up.

"Martin, stop that. It's a supporting wall. You bring that down, and you'll have the whole place down on us."

"What's the matter with you, are you chicken or something?" sneered Martin condescendingly, whacking at the wall with the lead piping and dislodging another brick in the process.

While this was going on, the bracelet had been furiously flashing a red warning at me. Several possible outcomes were running through my head, and none of them were good ones. The first time this had happened, Philip and I had tried together to discourage him but it had descended into an inevitable row, with Simon taking Martin's side.

Before long we were throwing the loose bricks Martin had dislodged from the wall at each other, which was when I had taken the blow to the temple, sending blood pouring everywhere, including into my eye. Only then did he stop, and it was just as well. The following day, what remained of the wall and the entire roof had collapsed.

Not wanting to repeat my trip to the hospital, I contemplated another choice. What if I simply left right now, without saying another word? I had my answer in an instant. The bracelet glowed red and I had a vision of me and Philip leaving, while Martin carried on his demolition job with Simon's assistance. The wall collapsed and both were crushed when the remainder of the roof caved in on them. Result? Both dead.

Great. I didn't have much in the way of options here, did I? It was no good coming back in time to avoid a gash on the head, but get two friends killed in the process? I'm sure that wasn't what the bracelet had been designed for. Somehow I had to try to stop him from causing any more damage at minimal risk to myself and the others.

Rather than get into the lengthy argument that would ultimately lead to the brick-throwing conflict, I decided I would have to take the bull by the horns and be authoritative from the start. It would probably get me thumped in the stomach or kicked in the shins by his steel-capped boots but that was better than stitches and a scar on my head for the rest of my life. So I went for it.

"He told you to stop. It's dangerous, so do as he said and stop now," I demanded, trying to sound tough and probably failing.

"Who's going to make me, you and whose army?" he shouted, an utterly predictable response.

It seemed I was left with no option. There was no way I would have been brave enough to do this the first time I was ten but with the benefit of experience, I decided that damage limitation was the order of the day. To his surprise, I ran across the room and cannoned into him, sending him flying to the ground and landing on the sodden mattress, which was soaked with rain and I don't even want to think what else. It stank.

It was just as well I had caught him off guard because attacking someone holding a length of metal pipe wasn't the brightest thing to do. Thankfully, he dropped that as we fell, immediately bringing his fists to bear, and I braced myself for what was coming next. And come it surely did, starting with a punch in the face that knocked me onto my back just as I was scrambling to get up. Then he kicked me twice in the ribs while I was lying on the floor, sending an agonising pain through my torso.

"You fucking wanker!" he exclaimed. "Who the fuck do you think you are?" We knew all the swear words by then, even if we didn't know what they meant. He cast his eye around looking for the lead pipe but he couldn't find it. I later found out that Philip had grabbed it and thrown it out the window during the scuffle. Then, to my relief, he said to the others, "I've had enough of this place. Come on, let's leave this dickhead here and go down the rec."

To my relief he stormed out, with the other two following him like lapdogs. I was a bit disappointed that Philip hadn't stayed because I thought he would support me on this one but he knew better than to get on Martin's wrong side when riled. I lay there for a while, in a puddle, waiting for the pain in my ribs to die down. He couldn't have been far off breaking one, as I was almost gasping for breath for the first minute or two before it began to subside.

I suppose it was a small price to pay for ensuring that nobody died. At least not yet. As a cold gust of wind swept through the derelict building, the crumbling walls shuddered in response to its icy touch. If the whole thing came down now and I perished here alone it would be an epic failure.

So, despite my discomfort, I hauled myself to my feet and hurried home as quickly as I could. There I threw myself on the mercy of my mother, who after scolding me for coming home in a mess and fighting, patched me up. After that, I headed off to my room to listen to some records until dinner was ready.

January's purchases were 'Fade to Grey' by Visage and the rather obscure 'I Am the Beat' by one-hit wonders, The Look. This was a rather unusual single because it had a loop at the end of the track which meant that instead of the record finishing, it kept repeating the words 'the beat' ad infinitum until I took the needle off.

As with all my records, I attached a note to each of them with a paperclip advising my future self not to throw them away. I had decided against stickers due to the risk of damage to the covers. The rest of my money I tended to spend on sweets. I had rediscovered my sweet tooth and indulged myself in everything from Fruit Salads to those candy imitation cigarettes which were freely available to kids at this time. Martin referred to them as starter fags, and claimed he had already tried a real one. Knowing him, he probably had.

I managed to earn a little extra money by doing jobs on the farm but it was still a pittance. With my knowledge of the future, I ought to be able to invest and return to the 2020s a millionaire. There was just one problem. How does a kid go about investing his princely savings of £3.58 when he hasn't even got a bank account? I couldn't even gamble my way to success. On Keith's advice, I had memorised a lot of sporting information before I had left but unfortunately, the village bookie didn't take bets off ten-year-olds.

I tried having a couple of pocket money bets directly with my friends, notably Martin, including an Oxford United game I had memorised the result of. Sadly, when I won he didn't pay up and just punched me in the stomach. Sometimes I wondered why I was even friends with him because it was becoming severely detrimental to my health.

As usual, what had happened at the old mill was all forgotten about by Monday morning at school when we were all friends again. However, it was mentioned again a few days later when news spread that the building had completely collapsed, and Martin realised that Philip and I had been right all along and he had been risking his life and ours. Then we got a mumbled, grudging acknowledgement which was about the closest we were ever going to get to an apology.

We found out about the mill roof caving in because Mr Jones, the headmaster, brought it up in assembly. He strongly hinted that he believed it was boys from the school who were responsible, taking the opportunity to give us all a lecture about it. He was brutally frank, pulling no punches when describing the danger of messing about in old buildings, adding an anecdote about a childhood friend who had died fooling around in a bombed-out house after the war.

Assembly was one of the few formal occasions that took place during our school day. I had not realised when I attended that our primary school was not like most others. I just assumed they were all the same. However, ours was one of a handful of experimental schools set up in the 1960s.

The concept was that rather than having formal classes with desks, everything should be open plan. There would be no timetables, outside of registration, assembly, and one or two specialist subjects. There were also no classrooms, just a large open-plan area divided into different sections for different activities, with small home pens in each corner. The idea was that, within reason, the children could just wander around and do what they wanted, when they wanted.

It wasn't quite as free as that sounds because the children would be guided by the teachers who would expect them to work on a minimum number of subjects each day and would advise on time management as required. So I couldn't just go into the art area and spend the entire day painting, never picking up a pen at all. They were very strong on handwriting, and we were expected to write every day, using only old-fashioned italic pens dipped in inkwells, with any mess absorbed by bright pink blotting paper. Biros were strictly frowned upon, seen as a modern menace that must never be allowed to pervade the school.

The same went for pocket calculators, which were also forbidden. The consensus was that if everyone started using them they would forget how to do basic mathematics. Looking at the modern world, I have to say they had a point. So it was long division, the old-fashioned way, something that I personally never had any problem with because I was years ahead of my age in mathematics.

There was a specific area of the room devoted to maths, just as there was for each of the core subjects. There would always be a teacher on hand who specialised in the subject in the vicinity, and they would wander around, dropping in on each child for a few minutes to discuss what they were working on and offer advice and support where required.

There was no school uniform at our school, another progressive idea, though most kids conformed to a standard outfit of trousers and a shirt for the boys, and a blouse and skirt for girls. At this time of year, most wore jumpers too, or even the dreaded tank tops, an unwelcome holdover from the 1970s. Fortunately, I had grown out of the only one I had ever been forced to wear, a revolting turquoise- and orange-striped monstrosity.

Having had all this freedom, it had come as a major and unwelcome shock when I moved up to my incredibly regimented secondary school. The two establishments could not have been more different, and having to adapt from one to the other did not serve me well. After the transition, I did not fulfil the potential of my early promise.

Being back here for a second crack at the educational cherry gave me a chance to reassess it all first-hand. Was this progressive schooling right for me, or not? In some ways, it was. It fostered a sense of self-reliance and self-discipline that I believe helped me to navigate my difficult teenage years. But having experienced such freedom it left me with a strong dislike of authority that followed me around for the rest of my life, leading to conflict both at school and in the workplace.

My mathematical abilities were picked up at a young age. Despite the open nature of the way we worked we were still subject to occasional tests, in which I invariably came out top. Unfortunately, by the age of eight I had finished all the Beta and Alpha maths textbooks in the school designed for kids up to eleven years old. After that, there was very little for me to do. No one was pushing me, and with no formal lessons, I did almost no maths for the next three years, halting my progress while everyone else caught up.

For children who were motivated and wanted to learn, being at the school was a generally positive experience. For those that didn't, I am not so sure. I wouldn't go so far as to say it was a slacker's paradise but it was very easy for those with little interest in education to coast along doing the bare minimum. Martin was a prime example.

Some activities, by their very nature, still had to take place at set times in set groups. P.E. was one of them. By far the most popular activity was football, and the school had a very enthusiastic teacher, Mr West, who managed all the school teams. I had fond memories of him as a thoroughly decent guy, the total opposite of his sadistic, evil equivalent at my next school.

I was pleased that Mr West shaped up to be every bit as dedicated and approachable as I remembered him, running every session with enthusiasm in his green tracksuit. I was thrilled when he chose me for the school team. I was just about good enough to get in, playing in midfield, but the star of the team was undoubtedly Martin. He played up front and scored a lot of goals, or at least he did until this final year of primary school. Then, his talents had been side-lined by a broken leg that put him out of action for the rest of the season. It also stopped him from fighting or causing any trouble for a few months, though when we went to separate schools in the autumn, hostilities between us hotted up.

In many ways, it was a relief when he broke his leg. After being on the receiving end of several knocks already since returning to 1981, I was positively looking forward to it. Having had a chance to retrospectively assess our friendship, I had concluded it was very one-sided and I don't know why I had put up with him for so long before.

Perhaps it was because I didn't know any different and had just assumed that getting beaten up was an occupational hazard of being a kid. But now I saw it differently and could see that I was getting the rough end of the stick. Yes, he was a friend to play with, and when he was on my side I had nothing to fear from anyone. But I had been on the receiving end of his anger once too often and enough was enough.

I had planned to let things play out without interfering when the day came that he broke his leg but those plans soon got thrown out of the window. On two successive nights, before we returned to school following the half-term break, I experienced extremely vivid dreams about the fate that was to befall him. Now, barely two weeks after the incident at the mill, I found myself facing another difficult decision.

I had previously only recalled scant details of what had happened during that fateful football match until my first dream, in which it was all played out in complete clarity. We had been taking part in the most important match for the team so far, the semi-final of the Oxfordshire Under-11's Cup, against the formidable Blackbird Leys. They had a reputation for being extremely rough opponents.

Late in the game, with the score at 1-1, we were awarded a corner and Martin was in the box, looking for an opportunity to score the winning goal. But he never got the chance. He might have been our best player and the hardest kid in our school but he was no match for the brutish central defender the opposition had brought along. It was very hard to believe he was an under-11 but there was no way to check since players weren't required to present their birth certificates. This lad must have been five and a half feet and fourteen stone at least, built more like a professional wrestler than a footballer. Consequently, we nicknamed him Giant Haystacks at half-time due to his resemblance to the TV wrestling star.

When Martin went up for the ball, Haystacks threw his full weight into hacking him down. We then winced at the sound of both his right tibia and fibula cracking. The game was held up as Martin was stretchered off in agony, and amazingly, the thug responsible wasn't even sent off. The referee, who was also the teacher in charge of the away team, claimed he hadn't seen it. With our star striker gone, the game went to extra time, and we ended up losing 2-1.

I wasn't sure what the significance of this dream was, all I knew was that when I woke up, the jewel was once again pulsing red at me. It was a warning and it was clear I was expected to do something to help Martin, but what, and why?

I got the answer the next night, in a second dream, which showed me an alternative version of events. This time, Martin avoided injury and it was we who had emerged victorious. We had gone on to play in the final, against North Leigh, at Oxford United's Manor Ground stadium. And we had won that too, lifting the trophy and celebrating as if we had just won the FA Cup.

The dream didn't end there. Martin had been spotted by talent scouts from the division three club at the final and went on to have a successful career, playing for them, as well as Derby County and Aston Villa. It was a far cry from the alternate future that I knew awaited him, where eventually his low-level delinquency would lead to him ending up in prison after a foolhardy and amateurish attempt to burgle the local post office at the age of eighteen.

The bracelet was glowing green when I woke up, suggesting that this was the correct direction the timeline should take. Frustratingly, what it had not offered me was any indication as to how I was to make this come about. The key moment where the injury would have occurred was missing from the dream. This annoyed me. Why make this more difficult than it needed to be? If it wanted me to change the timeline, it could at least have the decency to show me how to do it. Was it testing me in some way, to see if I was up to the task?

And quite frankly, why should I do it? After the way Martin had behaved towards me, why should I help him? Yes, he would have a better life, but he hardly deserved it. He wasn't the nicest person in the world by a long chalk, so what had he done to deserve the lavish lifestyle of a professional footballer? He would be hitting it big at just the right time too, his career taking off at the dawn of the Premier League when players were starting to make some serious money.

Then I thought about Mum and my prime reason for being here. I still had no idea how I was going to go about saving her but I knew it would require some sort of intervention. That reason alone was enough to make me decide to help Martin. If nothing else, it would provide some solid training and experience that might help me later.

The match was a home fixture on the field at the rear of our school, on a wet and cold Saturday morning. The pitch was an absolute quagmire after the wet winter and there wasn't a blade of grass to be seen in the area around the goalmouths, just a muddy mess. I was concerned that I wouldn't know when the right moment came before the game but thankfully the bracelet was getting inside my head and guiding me. I planned to wait for the crucial corner to come, then find a way to keep Haystacks and Martin apart.

We had already had a couple of corners during the second half but the bracelet, which I kept glancing at, wasn't indicating anything. I also wasn't getting the sense of urgency I had felt when Martin was risking bringing the roof of the old mill down on our heads. Then, finally, the moment arrived. We won another corner, the bracelet began flashing bright red, and I knew it was time to act. Firstly, I tried getting between the two of them, but that didn't work as there was a lot of jostling and shoving, including Haystacks using his suspiciously large muscles for an 'eleven-year-old' to bundle me out of the way.

This left me with only one course of action. The moment the corner kick was taken, I shoved Martin to the ground, out of harm's way, just as Haystacks was about to take him down. By a bizarre twist of fate, in the confusion the ball hit me on the head and rebounded between the goalposts. Without even trying, I had just scored the winning goal.

My teammates were jubilant but Martin was furious. Getting to his feet, he nearly went for me there and then. Once we were off the pitch, I got my reward for saving him from a horrible injury and setting him on the path to a rich and rewarding career, which was another smack in the face. I had no choice but to take it on the chin. I mean, what else could I do? There was no way I could explain any of this to him. I couldn't confide in anyone else, either. I wished I had someone to share all this with but I couldn't think of anyone who would take me seriously. All I could do was do my duty and move on.

That lunchtime, I walked home in the rain with a very sore jaw and a split lip. That's what you get for doing someone a good turn.

March 1981

By mid-March the sight of daffodils everywhere, blooms swaying in the stiff spring breeze, reminded me that the clock was ticking towards the day of Mum's fateful flight. I was now giving serious thought to what I could do to prevent it, coming up with numerous ideas before dismissing them as unworkable. I had only vague recollections of how she had come to be offered the trip to New York in the first place, not even remembering the name of the man who had proposed it.

All I could recall was that they had met at the village carnival where she always had a stall to promote her artwork. Unless I could stop her taking the stall it was difficult to see how I could prevent the encounter. I could beg her not to go, but what rationale would I have? As a last resort, I could try to physically stop her from going to the airport but it was hard to see how I was going to manage that in my puny child's body.

I tried asking the bracelet, even speaking to it out loud, in the hope that it would fill my head with the required information, but nothing was forthcoming. It didn't tend to respond to requests, only communicating information when it felt like it, and it wasn't ready to help me out just yet. I could only hope that when the time approached it would show me what to do, because if it didn't, I faced a very stiff task.

I wasn't at all happy with this need-to-know basis on which the bracelet operated. It made for a very one-sided relationship which I didn't feel was fair. If it could read my mind then it must have known how strongly I felt about all this, yet it seemed my feelings didn't come into account; I was here to do its bidding, not the other way around.

Thus far, the tasks I had been set had revolved around relatively minor events. Often weeks would go by where nothing happened at all but then why would it? I lived in the sticks, not some big city, and very little ever happened here. It made me wonder why I had been picked in the first place.

I watched the news with interest, but nothing particularly notable seemed to be going on in the early part of 1981, other than the creation of a new political party named the SDP, and the engagement of Prince Charles and Lady Diana. Of course I knew that wasn't going to have a happy ending, but from the bracelet's lack of interest, it seemed that event was part of the established timeline and would play out as it had before.

During those early months of 1981, I just got on with the business of living my ten-year-old life while I waited for the next task to come along. I often felt impatient because being young again wasn't all it was cracked up to be.

Apart from the initial excitement of rediscovering my childhood toys, I had little interest in childish pursuits once the novelty of playing around with a few plastic *Star Wars* figures wore off. The dark winter evenings could be pretty boring when I couldn't go out and do anything. I didn't miss the responsibility that came with adult life but I certainly missed the freedom.

What I did find enjoyable was immersing myself back into the music and television of the era. However, I could not always watch the programmes I wanted because, like many households, we only had one television set in the lounge. Only one channel could be watched at a time and we couldn't afford a video recorder. Very few people could. The only person I knew who had one was James Spencer, no surprise there.

My parents watched it most evenings during the winter. My mother liked to watch *Crossroads* and *Coronation Street*, neither of which appealed to me. Thankfully they weren't on nearly every night back then. Thursday was my favourite night because there were no soaps so I got to watch *Tomorrow's World* and *Top of the Pops*, which I loved having the chance to see again. *Tomorrow's World* was fascinating viewing for a time traveller, watching to see which of their predictions had come true and which they had got spectacularly wrong.

After school, I got the television to myself. Dad would still be at work and Mum would be cooking so I could watch children's TV. This was well-made, quality stuff in this era, infinitely superior to the endless daytime dross which would eventually displace it from BBC1. The likes of Johnny Ball, Johnny Morris, and others made programmes for kids that were genuinely entertaining, thought-provoking, and worth staying in after school for. And then, there was *Grange Hill*.

I found this show fascinating as a kid because it gave me my first glimpse into a world of schooling very different from the progressive environment which was all I had known. While I enjoyed the antics of Tucker and his mates, I also found the portrayal of secondary school quite daunting. The show didn't pull any punches when it came to tackling the harsh realities of life, with the character of Gripper Stebson being particularly terrifying. If this was what St Jacob's, the secondary school in our village, was like, it was going to be a shock to the system when I got there.

I never did get there though, nor to any other secondary school remotely resembling that portrayed in the show. Simon, who was already at St Jacob's, assured me that it was not a million miles away from *Grange Hill*. But I was not destined to find this out for myself, as unbeknown to me, I was already being lined up to take a different path.

I am sure those involved did it with the best intentions. It was to give me the chance of a better future, I was told, but the implications of the impact it would have on my personal development had not been taken into consideration. I cannot really blame my parents or teachers for that because records show that children who attend private schools get better academic results and go on to high-flying, well-paid careers. Whether or not it makes them nicer or more well-rounded individuals is another matter entirely. They were not thinking that far ahead when the prospect of me attending Wolfminster School became a possibility.

Wolfminster was one of the most prestigious schools in the country as well as being one of the most exclusive. Tucked away among the gleaming spires in the heart of Oxford, its secretive, publicity-shy nature gave it an air of mystique. That was if you had even heard of it. Unlike some of the other well-known fee-paying schools in Oxford, such as Magdalen College School and St Edward's, Wolfminster kept a very low profile.

It was much smaller than those other schools, for a start. It took a roll of just twenty-four pupils in each year in a single class. There were even fewer in the sixth form, making for a total of 160 pupils, all boys. The fees were eye-watering, even exceeding those of Eton and Harrow. The children that went there were highly privileged and in most cases from wealthy stock. There was even a tinge of blue blood here and there. Until I started rubbing shoulders with these toffs I hadn't understood what the expression 'being born with a silver spoon in your mouth' meant, but it didn't take long to find out.

To be fair, some of the kids were genuinely bright and did go on to achieve great things in the world of science. Those tended to be the quieter, more bookish types and were generally amenable. But as for some of the others, I don't know where to start.

They were the ones who were there on Daddy's money alone. They did not need to achieve great academic results when the family firm was already being lined up, ready for them to take over. Some of the others went into politics and became MPs, laughably trying to present themselves as men of the people. The truth was that they hadn't done an honest day's work in their lives or anything that would enable them to understand or even care about the lives of ordinary people.

They led pampered, sheltered lives that led to a particular kind of superior arrogance which is very hard to combat if they consider you to be a pleb. That was their favoured word for anyone they evaluated as being below their social class, which was practically everyone. I wondered how the likes of them would have fared if thrust into a school like *Grange Hill*, full of Gripper Stebsons. They wouldn't have lasted five minutes.

So how on earth did I, from a long line of country farming folk, end up there? Well, it was all down to changes in legislation, the details of which I didn't fully comprehend. I am not sure if it was a national policy or a local council initiative but the crux of the matter was that the school was now required to take one local pupil from a working-class background on a scholarship each year, plus three others at vastly reduced fees.

I later found out that the school was all in favour of this as the scholarship was tax deductible in some convoluted way. In other words, it was beneficial to them financially so they were more than happy to go along with it.

Was it beneficial to the 'lucky' student awarded that free place? Most outside observers would believe it was, seeing it as the opportunity of a lifetime. But they couldn't see the school from the inside. Nobody could unless they were part of it. Just as one of the privileged kids from Wolfminster would have been a fish out of water in a school like Grange Hill, the reverse was also true.

Every primary school in the county was invited to put up one candidate to sit an entrance exam, from which the scholarship and three other places would be selected. I was chosen from my school largely due to my mathematical excellence.

On the day of the exam, over two hundred boys turned up and crowded into the school's chapel, known for some undetermined reason as Big John. Peculiar room names were common around the school. In most cases the origins of these were lost in the mists of time as the school had been there a long time, able to trace its origin back to the mid-fourteenth century, making it one of the oldest in the country.

I was as amazed as anyone when I won the scholarship and subsequently found myself thrust into this strange world of cloisters and mortarboards. It wasn't long before I was made painfully aware I did not belong, not only by the other kids but by many of the masters too. The school did not use the term 'teacher' as I was told that was just for common people at common schools. Also, the boys were only ever referred to by their surnames. I was Taylor from the day I started to the day I left. Most of the kids never even learned my first name.

Some of the boys could be cruel but the worst abuse and sadism came from some of the masters. They had been getting away with it for decades and their practices put schoolboy bullying in the shade. And so began five years of abject misery, not helped by coming into the school still reeling from the aftermath of losing one parent and the revelation that my cousin was now shagging the other.

To the posh kids at the school, I was the country bumpkin to be ridiculed at every opportunity. Yet cruelly, back home, I was to suffer the reverse fate. I was disowned by my former friends who now considered me to be the snobby posh kid who thought he was too good for his old mates.

This came to a head only a few weeks into my first term when a group of them, including Martin, waited for me to get off the bus from Oxford and then jumped me. They tore the badge off my outrageously expensive maroon and cream blazer, before pushing me into the pond on the village green. It was then, in a moment of despair, that I realised I didn't belong anywhere, anymore. I had no mother, no friends, and a father who was too smitten by his young lover to care about what I was going through. This went on for five years, until at sixteen, I jumped ship and went to the local college of further education where I was much happier.

Before the end of the first month, I had barely scratched the surface of the horrors going on at the school, but I already knew that going there had been the worst move of my life. It had been a decision made with good intentions but with no knowledge of what I was letting myself in for. No one in the village knew anyone who had ever been there, so there was no precedent. But I survived, somehow. And now, here I was facing the entrance examination for a second time. It was the perfect opportunity to change my future for the better. All I had to do was mess up the exam and that would be it. No more Wolfminster.

That was the plan, from the moment I was called into the meeting at school with my parents and Mr Jones at the beginning of March. This was when the idea was first broached. He explained that the exam was towards the end of the month and he would like to put me forward.

My parents reacted enthusiastically to the news, particularly Mum who was all for people trying to better themselves. Unlike Edith and William, she had ambition, always hoping that one day her art would bear fruit. I couldn't blame her for wanting the best for me and she couldn't have known what the implications were. I could see by the excited and surprised looks on both my parents' faces, as Mr Jones explained what all this entailed, that neither of them had ever heard of Wolfminster before.

How was I to react? I could hardly say there and then in the meeting that Wolfminster was a hellhole and I wanted nothing to do with it. They would want to know how I could know that, which wasn't something I could easily explain. Instead, I went along with it for a while to buy some time.

The truth was, I didn't even know if I could pass the entrance exam. I had managed to get by in primary school these past couple of months but I had been humbled to discover that it was all a lot harder than I expected.

The problem was that I had forgotten huge chunks of what I had learned in school in the intervening forty years. Some things were not a problem – I don't think people ever forget staples like times tables – but a lot of other stuff such as basic science and history had gone clean out of my head. Even some of the maths I had forgotten, like the names of the different types of triangles and shapes, and I was supposed to be a genius at that. Eventually, I came to the depressing conclusion that I was dumber at fifty than I had been at ten.

March slipped by while I weighed up my options. It was a pretty month in Meadowbrook Lane. Not only was the grass bank next to the brook brimming with daffodils, but the trees began to blossom too, flowering in appreciation of the warming days and the lengthening hours of daylight. As the end of the month and the exam approached, I became increasingly in two minds about the situation, because around the time we passed the spring equinox, the bracelet decided to venture an opinion on the matter.

I had been playing out scenarios in my mind, wondering how life might play out differently if I went to St Jacob's, when the warning red glow started. And every time I thought about messing up the exam, it did the same thing.

"Why?" I blurted out loud, in a private moment in my room. "Why do you want me to go there?"

I wasn't expecting it to talk to me, it didn't do that, but at least it could have given me some sort of sign now it had raised the issue. But no, it just sat on my wrist in sullen silence as it often did. Why did it have to play these games? Perhaps it would throw me a vision at the last minute like it had previously but I hated having to act on the hoof all the time.

Then the dreams started again. At night, I began to picture scenarios played out at Wolfminster that I didn't want to see. At first, I thought perhaps some of these were memories that were so horrific that I had somehow suppressed them, burying them so deep within my mind that they could never be unearthed again.

Soon, I realised that much of what I was dreaming related to events I had not been privy to. They involved other kids and masters, and whilst not explicit, some of what was implied I could scarcely bring myself to think about the next day. I thought my time at the school had been bad but it paled in comparison to what others had been through.

The school was rife with abuse, both physical and sexual. There were also hints of cover-ups, mysterious disappearances, and possible murders. I used to think that *Inspector Morse* was far-fetched with so much skulduggery going on among the cloisters but after these dreams perhaps I ought to reassess that position. It left me with a difficult decision to make. It was clear what the bracelet wanted me to do. It wanted me to pass the exam, go to Wolfminster, and tackle some of these issues.

How I was expected to do this wasn't clear. I would be eleven by the time I went there, going up against people stronger, better financed, and in positions of power, even if I did have the benefit of inside information. I would undoubtedly also be putting myself in a lot of danger. If what I had seen of the P.E. master there was true, I didn't want to get anywhere near him.

I didn't want to go near the place, full stop. If I went to Wolfminster again I would be choosing a path which had previously done me no good whatsoever.

Then again, perhaps this time it could all be different. Last time, I had gone in there completely unprepared with not a clue about what I was letting myself in for. This time I knew what to expect and could prepare. I would also have the bracelet to guide me through any sticky situations, at least for the first term. Perhaps I could turn this whole thing to my advantage and do some good for others too.

The bracelet certainly thought so, showing its appreciation of my change of heart with a light green glow. It seemed it had made my mind up for me. I was going to have to take the exam and hope that my rusty fifty-year-old brain was still capable of passing it.

On the day of the exam, Dad drove me into Oxford in his green Morris Marina van. This was a tradesman's version of one of British Leyland's unfashionable 1970s cars which he used for his carpentry business. At that time it was still possible to drive around most of Oxford unhindered, apart from Cornmarket Street and Queen Street. These were closed to normal traffic, which was just as well as they were so clogged up with buses most of the time that there wasn't room for anything else.

The school did not announce its presence in any way and the first time we went there we struggled to find it. It was located just off Merton Street in a part of Oxford which will be familiar to anyone who has ever watched films or television shows set in the city. With undergraduates cycling past in mortarboards and gowns, this picturesque place was an obvious choice for makers of the period drama, *Brideshead Revisited,* to film without having to make too many alterations to make it look like the 1920s. Most of that filming had taken place over the past year or so for broadcast later in 1981.

It was here that the way into Wolfminster could be found. The entrance was a subtle, unassuming affair, in keeping with the secretive nature of its existence, located on a narrow lane tucked away between two colleges. Entry was through a single, wrought iron black gate in an archway made of weathered stone, with only a small metal plaque on the wall to indicate that there was a school there at all.

Both sides of the archway were carved ornately into shapes of menacing-looking gargoyles, a feature that could be found on ancient buildings in many places in

Oxford. It brought to mind the line 'abandon hope all ye who enter here'. It was certainly an apt quote in my case.

The gate led across a small cobbled courtyard to a cluster of buildings, most of which were completely out of sight of the lane. There was very little in the way of open space. There was no proper playground and no sports fields. Instead, the school had free access to the university's facilities.

There was also no facility for car parking, at least not on site, so we had parked at the Westgate Shopping Centre. This was probably a good thing as I can't imagine the Marina making a good impression. I had no idea where the masters parked their cars if they even had any. I had seen some of them riding around on ancient pushbikes, whereas others, particularly the older ones, never seemed to leave the premises at all. It was as if they were part of the very fabric of the place.

One couldn't help but be overawed by the sense of antiquity and history that pervaded the place when first encountering it. Walking across the cobbles now, even I felt nostalgic despite having grown to loathe the place, those thoughts were quickly vanquished as we were greeted at the door by one of the most fearsome masters of all. This was Doctor Runcible, the history master, who was known to the boys as Rasputin.

He was smiling like a devil in disguise as he greeted us at the door, with no indication of the psychotic tendencies he would display when there were no parents around. Many other boys were arriving at the same time so Rasputin directed us down a narrow corridor to where we needed to go. I, of course, already knew the way.

We were heading to Big John, the converted chapel, its former pews now repurposed as austere school desks. A cold, uncomfortable ambience permeated the room, lit only by the dim light filtering through ancient stained glass and the flames of several candles. These were set in solid gold candelabras behind the lectern from which the school's resident chaplain, Reverend Philips, dispensed fire and brimstone to the 'wicked' children every morning. Kev the Rev, as he was nicknamed, was a formidable figure but thankfully there was no sign of him today.

It was not a large room by any means, and with around two hundred kids in attendance today, we were packed in like sardines onto the hard wooden pews which numbed your arse if you sat on them for any length of time. There were no cushions because Kev the Rev didn't believe his flock to be worthy of them. They were expected to suffer for their sins and besides, cushions would be an extravagant expense. Despite the massive fees paid by the parents of most of the pupils here, precious little of that cash found its way down to them in the way of creature comforts.

At least today I didn't have to mingle with any of the stuck-up twats that would later be my classmates. The others present were all normal primary school kids, aged ten and eleven, like me. Yes, they were brainy, that's how they had got here, but at least most of them were from working-class or middle-class backgrounds. Most of them would be unlucky today, and go home empty-handed. Or lucky, depending on your point of view.

There were no individual desks in front of the pews, just a long unbroken shelf which was barely wide enough to squeeze a piece of A4 paper onto. We were packed in so closely it would have been easy to copy off the next person. This wasn't an appropriate place to hold an exam at all, but it was where I had taken my O-Levels. Admittedly, then there had been only twenty-four of us so we had been a little more spaced out.

Dad left me at the door, after which we got an introduction from the headmaster, who was known simply as The Master. The name always prompted thoughts of the renegade Time Lord from *Doctor Who*, who only the previous Saturday I had watched chuckling as he caused Tom Baker to fall off a tower and regenerate.

To be fair to Mr Miller, known by the nickname of 'Windy', courtesy of *Camberwick Green*, he was quite affable by the standards of most of the teaching staff. After he had waffled on for ages about the tradition and history of the school, as befitted his nickname, the exam papers were produced and we all got on with it.

The paper was split into three sections, the first two of which, maths and English, seemed straightforward enough. It was when I saw the third part that I began to panic. It took the form of a general knowledge quiz, encompassing bits of history, geography, science, and various other things. Much of it was advanced stuff, way beyond the scope of what was taught up to the age of eleven but perhaps that was the point. They wanted to sort out the wheat from the chaff.

I knew that I had known a lot of this stuff in the past, thanks to the naturally inquisitive mind I had as a child. That was how I had passed the first time. But as I had already discovered at primary school, forty years is a long time to be expected to remember such things.

The first section was science and I was stumped by the opening question which was 'Which element has the chemical symbol Hg?' I knew I used to know this because science was something I had been interested in. I even had a big book all about it at home that I had eagerly devoured as a kid. But I hadn't looked at it since I had returned to 1981 and as I looked at the question now, the answer would not come to me.

Then the bracelet pulsed green and the word 'mercury' popped into my head just like that. And so it went on throughout the paper, giving me the names of everything from the capital of Mozambique to the name of Henry VIII's third wife.

I was relieved to discover that I didn't need help for every question, which reassured me that I hadn't become a total ignoramus. But the bracelet's help was very welcome with the rest of it. As cheating devices went it was the ultimate tool, providing all the answers and invisible to everyone but me. There was no doubting its agenda. It was determined that I was going to attend this school.

At the end of the test, we were thanked and then briefly shown around the rest of the school, where I got my first glimpse of the pupils already in attendance. They were on their lunch break and exactly as I remembered them, sneering and entitled as they looked down their noses at us commoners. As for lunch, we didn't get offered any, which was perhaps just as well. If I had been under the impression that it would be all caviar and canapes at a school that charged ten grand a term, then those illusions were well and truly shattered when I started.

People probably ate better in prison.

April 1981

"Miss, why have you only given me three out of ten?" I protested, badgering my teacher after she handed me back my creative writing book.

It was the last day of school before the Easter holidays, and I had been very excited about the current half-term project. The topic was 'What will life be like in the year 2000?' There had been several circle time discussions on the matter, art projects mainly involving spaceships, and story-writing, plus we were all expected to write a non-fiction piece setting out what we thought the future would be like, and why.

This was tailor-made for me – after all, I had already seen it. What could possibly go wrong? So I wrote what I thought was a very articulate piece heralding the rise of the mobile phone and the internet, amongst other things.

I was slightly wary that I might be leaving a written copy of something incriminating that could be found later containing information that no one could have known in 1981. Nonetheless I went ahead, just keeping certain details vague. I did not, for example, include the names of companies like eBay and Google. Instead, I just described the nature of how they worked.

Miss Bakewell was not impressed, much to my annoyance. I took her dismissal of my ideas to heart so much that I decided to take her to task over it. She was generally quite amenable during the weekly individual reviews she had with each child in her group. Therefore, I was hopeful she would give me a decent explanation. She was young and still full of the enthusiasm that people in most professions have in the early part of their careers. Anyway, I was curious to find out why she had given me such a low score. It was unprecedented for me.

"They were interesting ideas," she began, "but not exactly imaginative. You say that the world will be much as it is now – people eating the same things, still using motor cars and watching television. The only new concept you've come up with is this internet thing. As you know, we've got the Commodore PET in the audio/visual lounge but the idea of everybody having one and them all being linked up? That's a bit far-fetched, don't you think? I mean look at the cost for a start. We were very lucky to get ours – most schools cannot afford one."

"It's new technology. They will get much cheaper. Look how expensive televisions were when they first came out. Now everybody can afford one. Also, you are being contradictory. First, you said I'm not imaginative, then you dismissed my internet idea as far-fetched."

Most other teachers would have ticked me off at this point for being disrespectful but to be fair, she continued to give me the time of day.

"I just think that after all the discussion we've had this term your ideas might have been a little more futuristic. I mean, take Carey for example. She's written about how there won't be any need for food anymore and we'll be able to get all our nutritional content from just a few small pills."

"And you think people will go for that, do you? A little tablet rather than a nice roast dinner or steak and chips?"

I was worried I might be pushing my luck but she remained receptive, conceding, "That's a fair point. What about transport, though? Some of the others wrote about how we'll all be travelling around in electric flying cars, eliminating traffic jams and pollution forever."

"Do you honestly believe we'll develop flying cars in less than twenty years?" I asked.

"I don't see why not. I mean look how short a time it took to get from the Wright Brothers' first flight to aeroplanes fighting in the skies during the First World War. Barely a decade."

"And what about the practicalities?" I asked. "All those cars flying around all over the place with no roads. How are we going to stop them from crashing into each other? It'll be carnage."

"Oh, I daresay they'll develop technology to overcome that. Speaking of technology, you haven't included anything about robots, either. A lot of the other children were very keen on them."

"That's because there won't be any."

"Well, that's not what Philip thinks. He wrote about how we'll all be living lives of luxury with incredible life-like androids doing all the work and catering to our every need."

"Philip is wrong. I expect he said we'll all be living on Mars too, right?"

"As a matter of fact, he did. Surely you can't deny that we're going to spread out into space. I mean look where we are already – it's less than a quarter of a century since we first sent Sputnik into orbit. Since then we've been to the moon, and this Sunday, NASA is going to launch the first-ever space shuttle – the ship that's going to revolutionise space travel."

"Yes – until they start blowing up. I don't want to disappoint you, but I think the space race has gone as far as it's going to go. In fact, I confidently predict we won't set foot on the moon again for at least forty years. As for living on other planets, the costs of that would be astronomical, and it would also be completely impractical. It's never going to happen."

"I'm sorry, Nick, but I am incredibly disappointed in your lack of imagination for this topic. That's why I've only given you three out of ten. You're going to have to buck your ideas up when you go to Wolfminster, you know."

By now, the offer of my scholarship had come through and against my better judgement, I had accepted it. I was trying to keep it quiet but that was proving to be impossible. The teachers were all aware and I knew my parents had told the other aunts and uncles. It wouldn't be long until it filtered through to the rest of my classmates and I wasn't looking forward to that. In my previous life, Martin had been out of action during this period with a broken leg. Now, thanks to my earlier intervention he was very much still at large and therefore dangerous. I wasn't expecting a positive reaction from him.

I couldn't be bothered to argue with Miss Bakewell any longer, so I headed back out to the open plan area where the final day play sessions were well underway. It was a tradition in our school that on the last day of term the children were allowed to bring games in, and there was an impressive collection of what, to my eyes, was effectively memorabilia. Philip had brought in KerPlunk which had attracted quite a crowd. However, I was more interested in thrashing a few unsuspecting classmates in a game of Monopoly.

I suppose I would sound as if I was bragging if I claimed that I was very good at this game because it allowed me to put my mathematical prowess to good use. The thing I love about Monopoly is that it has got the mixture of skill and luck exactly right. Games of pure chance like Snakes and Ladders hold no attraction to me as it's just random who wins.

In Monopoly, the luck of the dice plays a part but poor luck can be overcome with superior strategy. The same is said of poker, but that's a game I never had any joy with. Even though I know the odds of the different hands, I've always been terrible at it. Perhaps I give too much away with my body language. It's a shame I never managed to master it considering the eye-watering sums on offer in those big tournaments in Las Vegas. But Monopoly? That was my game.

One of the kids from Mr West's group had brought in a set, so I joined in with three others, using my favourite piece, the dog. Things didn't start too promisingly, with a couple of bad Chance cards, but I soon began to turn things around. By sticking to my key strategy, of getting three houses on a set of properties as soon as possible, I was able to clean up. I figured out at an early age by studying the increments of rent on the cards that three is the magic number.

After school, I headed home for the two weeks of the Easter break. I always looked forward to this holiday as it often coincided with the first decent spell of weather of the year. That was true of this year when it fell later in April. The date hadn't escaped Edith's notice as she was fussing around my mother in the kitchen when I got home. She seemed to spend more time in our house than her own these days.

"Ooh, isn't Easter late this year?" she was saying as I came in. It was a completely pointless remark in my opinion but utterly predictable out of Edith's mouth. You would have thought at her age that she would have got used to the date moving around each year, especially with her Christian faith. I didn't feel like getting involved in the conversation so I offered a brief greeting before heading up to my room. As I climbed the stairs I heard my mother say, "So, Julia can't do it? Oh, that's a shame. Maybe I could ask Tracy."

Ask Tracy what? I wondered, as I reached my room and put a purchase from the previous week, 'Reward' by The Teardrop Explodes, on the turntable. Whatever it was, if it involved Tracy it couldn't be good.

I was right. I had forgotten that Saturday was my parents' wedding anniversary and they were going out for a meal at the Berni Inn, of all places. This ivy-clad building on the edge of the village was a former coaching inn that had been converted to provide an exquisite culinary experience that was considered the height of sophistication in our humble rural backwater.

All I could remember people doing in the future was taking the piss out of Berni Inns, claiming that all they sold were prawn cocktails, steak and chips, and Black Forest gateau. I think they were doing them an injustice because there was a lot more on the menu than that. The founders, Frank and Aldo Berni, had pioneered the idea of the chain restaurant in the UK, creating the template for all the Harvesters, Beefeaters, and countless others that would imitate the design later. As a child, a meal out at one, in an era when few restaurants catered for children, was something special.

I wasn't going to be indulged this weekend, and as I soon discovered, Tracy was to be my babysitter for the evening. Being babysat by anyone other than my sister was a relatively new experience for me, starting only after she went off to university. Since Linda hadn't come home for Easter, informing us instead that she was spending the break in the south of France, someone else had to be found. On the previous couple of occasions that I had needed a sitter, Julia had done it, but this weekend she was on a work outing. So the job was passed to Tracy.

I knew as soon as it was mentioned that something was afoot. The bracelet began pulsing its familiar red warning light but further information was not forthcoming. I vaguely remember something about Tracy looking after me forty years ago but couldn't recall anything notable about it. This time I would have my wits about me, so if she was up to anything, I'd find out.

I tried to prevent Tracy from coming by suggesting that I could go and spend the evening at the farmhouse with my grandparents. That idea was rejected as being too late for them, as the table was booked for 8pm and they liked to go to bed early. So, home alone with Tracy I was destined to be.

It didn't escape my notice on the night that she had come dressed similarly to New Year again. When she complimented Dad on his suit, without commenting on Mum's dress, her intentions couldn't have been more blatant but my mother seemed oblivious. Perhaps it was because I had the benefit of foresight whereas she wouldn't even have contemplated that her husband might have an affair with his niece. That sort of thing didn't go on in Meadowbrook Lane.

I thought they both looked very smart. Most people took a lot more pride in their appearance in 1981 than they did forty years later. It was likely that everyone in the Berni Inn tonight would be wearing their Sunday best. It was a far cry from families wandering into inferior chains in the future in their jeans and joggers, as their kids ran around the indoor play area causing havoc. My father had even put a flower in his buttonhole, giving the impression that he was off to a wedding rather than going out for a steak.

Tracy was all sweetness and light, to begin with – at least while my parents were still there.

"We should be back about eleven," said Mum, as they headed towards the front door. "There's some cooked ham in the fridge and a fresh loaf in the tin – feel free to help yourself to a sandwich if you get hungry."

"That's very kind of you, Aunt Mary," gushed Tracy, as if she were some sweet and innocent young thing.

"And help yourself to a drink too. There's some lemonade in the fridge."

"Have fun," added my father, looking appreciatively at Tracy. I don't know what he meant by that but it was obvious from the way Tracy flashed her eyes back at him what sort of fun they were thinking about. But still, my mother seemed oblivious.

When Julia looked after me, we played games or watched TV together. But the second my parents were out the door it became clear there was going to be none of that tonight. Tracy made a beeline straight for the drinks on the sideboard and poured herself a neat vodka.

"What do you think you're doing?" I asked, following her in.

"Shut it, pipsqueak," she countered, taking a swig from the crystal tumbler. "Didn't you hear what your mum said? Help yourself to a drink."

"Yes, and I'm pretty sure she said lemonade."

"Perhaps she did, but if you remember, I was eighteen a couple of weeks ago. That makes me a responsible adult."

"An adult, maybe. I don't know about responsible."

"I'm responsible for you. I'm the grown-up and you're the kid. So you do what I say," she said, pouting as she reached into the pocket of her leather jacket and pulled out a packet of cigarettes.

"Let's see what's on the telly," she said, wandering over to the box in the corner and pressing the on switch. While she was waiting for it to warm up, she lit up, before slumping down on the sofa."

"Mum doesn't like people smoking in here," I said.

"I didn't see her complaining at New Year when Uncle Henry was stinking the place out with his pipe," she said.

"That was a party," I replied.

"Yes, well, so's this," she said, glancing at the screen which was showing a dramatic cinematic scene of a volcano erupting. "It's a private party, and only I'm invited. So you can fuck off to your bedroom."

"What?" I said, shocked that she would use language like that to a ten-year-old.

"You heard me. I'm the babysitter and I'm in charge. And I've decided that your bedtime is 8pm. So off you pop and go to bed or have a bath or something. You can do that on your own, can't you?"

"Of course I can," I replied.

"Good, because I've no desire to see your wee willie winkie," she said crudely, taking a drag followed by a sip of vodka.

Before I could stop myself I blurted out, "I bet you'd like to see my dad's, though, wouldn't you?"

Her cocky demeanour vanished. She leapt up, put the ciggie down on a glass ashtray, and got up close and personal, invading my personal space.

"What's that supposed to mean? Been spying on me, have you, you little perv?"

"Why? Got something to hide? I saw the way you looked at my dad earlier."

Standing right in front of me, vodka still in her right hand, she slapped me across the cheek with her left, making a resounding thwack as she made contact. That, I had not been expecting. The bracelet hadn't tipped me off about this specifically but since it had been red all evening, I guess it was a general warning that nothing good was going to come of tonight.

I recoiled, feeling a sharp sting spreading across the right side of my face.

"And there's more where that came from if you don't keep your fucking nose out of my business, you little shit."

"I'll tell Mum," I said.

"Like she's going to believe you. All she's interested in is her crappy paintings. What if I was fucking your dad? She probably wouldn't notice even if we were at it on your kitchen table. Now get out of my sight and if you mention any of this to anyone, I swear I will fucking kill you."

"Fine," I said, conceding temporary defeat. I was wise enough to realise that this was not the time to escalate the confrontation. It would be far better to back down for now and let her think she had won. Then I could withdraw and regroup.

Without a further word, I went up to my room and waited. I could hear her downstairs, laughing as she watched whatever was on the telly. She didn't seem remotely fazed by our conversation which suggested she didn't regard me as any sort of threat. That was a good thing. It was always better in these situations to be underestimated. Either that or she was just drunk,

I went to have a bath and examined my cheek in the bathroom mirror while I was running the water. It was red and still smarted but there was no long-lasting sign of injury. I was relieved about that. The last thing I wanted was my mother to see it and question me about it, though I suppose if she did I could just say Martin did it. Hopefully, it would all look normal in the morning.

I might have retreated upstairs but I wasn't done with the detective work yet, not by a long chalk. I was curious to see what interaction would occur when my parents got home.

They came in just after eleven, both sounding quite tipsy. They would have shared a bottle of wine at the Berni, maybe two. I huddled out of sight at the top of the stairs and listened to some small talk between the three of them. Then my name was mentioned.

"Has Nick been OK?" asked Mum.

"As good as gold," she replied. "He went to bed about ten and when I looked in on him about twenty minutes ago he was fast asleep."

Liar – she had not once been upstairs.

"Well, I guess I ought to see Tracy home," said Dad. "I know it's only three doors down, but you can't be too careful these days, can you, not after all that Ripper business. I know they've caught him now but you never know what other nutters might be about."

Mum agreed to this so they went outside, and she went into the kitchen. The bracelet glowed green, hinting to me that the coast was clear if I wanted to follow them. Now was my chance to see for myself what was going on. His offer to walk her home alone was damning enough. He had never offered to do that with Julia and she lived further down the lane than Tracy

I slipped down the stairs, taking care not to tread on the creaky step, then sneaked outside, still in my pyjamas. It was a clear and cold night so I didn't want to be out in it too long, especially with no shoes on. But before I went back in I was determined to see what the two of them were up to.

They were walking up ahead, with arms linked, giggling, and stumbling slightly, both in a state of inebriation. As they passed Brenda's house I heard Tracy say, "No need to worry about her, the nosey old bitch will be in bed by now."

I stayed well back, not wanting to be seen, taking advantage of trees, cars, and the sides of the cottages to stay hidden. It wasn't difficult as there was no street lighting on the lane, only what was coming from the houses and from the moon, which was about two-thirds full. I didn't have a good view of them until they approached her house where the outside light had been left on, presumably in preparation for her return.

I took cover outside Honeysuckle, crouching down behind Stan's Morris Traveller and then I saw what I already knew was inevitable. Even so, I was shocked by how brazen they were.

The two of them were snogging and groping at each other by the side of her house. It was bad enough when I saw one hand on her breasts but when I realised he had the other one right up her skirt, I had to look away. There was no denying what he was doing, and she was well into it, gasping and moaning like a porn star. And on his wedding anniversary, too. It made a mockery of his marriage.

Then they leapt apart as I heard William's voice calling out, "Tracy, is that you?"

My dad scarpered, running away and right past my position but he didn't spot me crouched behind the car.

William didn't see him either as he opened the front door to let Tracy in. Had he heard anything? He must have heard something or he wouldn't have come out. No doubt she would make some excuse – blame it on a cat or something.

I remained rooted to the spot, devastated by what I had just seen. Why I should react like that I did not know, because it wasn't as if I hadn't known it was coming. I suppose it was seeing it confirmed, quite literally in the flesh, that had brought the reality of it all home.

The thing that hurt the most was that all of this was months before my mother was due to get on that plane. It made a mockery of his later claim that he had turned to Tracy for comfort after her death. I had always suspected that to be a lie. The only crumb of comfort I could draw from it was that at least Mum hadn't known anything about it. Well, if I had anything to do with it, she was going to know about it this time, long before the subject of New York arose.

My immediate priority was to get back indoors undetected, and I was worried that Dad might have locked the front door. Thankfully, when I tried it I found he had not. We still lived in a time when people in the lane generally felt no need to. Even so, I didn't go in straight away despite the cold seeping into my bones. They might still be downstairs. I gave it five minutes and then slowly opened the door and let myself in.

There was no sign of either of them which suggested they had gone upstairs. I was worried they might have looked in my room to check on me but clearly they hadn't or they would be looking for me now. I was safely back inside without anyone knowing I had been gone.

But my relief at getting back in undetected soon evaporated when I realised what was happening upstairs.

I didn't think things could get any worse, after the evening I'd just had, but I was wrong. As I crept back upstairs, I heard something no one ever wants to hear – the sound of my parents having sex.

This really was the lowest of the low. My father had got all turned on by Tracy fooling around outside, then come back feeling horny and immediately jumped on my mother to satisfy his urges.

This was about as sleazy as it was possible to get.

May 1981

I couldn't face my parents the day after what I had seen and heard that night so I headed up to the farmhouse to spend some time with Jack and Nellie. They were always pleased to see their grandchildren, and enjoying some quality time with them helped to take my mind off things for a few hours.

At teatime we watched the launch of the first-ever space shuttle, which Jack confidently proclaimed would herald the beginning of a great new era for space travel. What he didn't know was that this shuttle would be one of two that would blow up in the years ahead, killing all on board. But there was no need to tell him that. Both he and Nellie were as optimistic about the future as Miss Bakewell and my classmates had been during our Year 2000 project.

I didn't have the heart to tell them that far from being an exciting new dawn, the world would go steadily downhill after that milestone date. In my opinion, anyway. Mercifully, neither of them would be around to witness that decline.

Nellie fancied herself as a bit of a clairvoyant and was always reading tea leaves and palms, as well as checking out her horoscope. One day during the Easter holidays, she offered to read mine, confidently declaring that I would live a long and happy life. I'm convinced that was the stock answer she gave to everyone because if she even had a glimpse of what lay ahead, she would not be making such rosy predictions. Of course, her prophecy could still come true but it would all come down to my interventions rather than anything written in the stars.

The confirmation of what was going on between Tracy and my father hadn't changed anything yet because only I knew about it. I couldn't confide in anyone from the family because I knew I wouldn't be taken seriously. Instead I bided my time, spent as much time at the farmhouse as possible, and mulled it over. The deadline to act was looming, and I would need to come up with a plan soon because I couldn't be sure that I could rely on the bracelet when the time came.

I was sad when the school holidays ended because the two weeks in the company of Jack and Nellie had been well spent. I visited them far more than any of the other grandchildren did, and they liked nothing better than to talk about the old days. I spent many an hour in the large kitchen listening to Nellie reminiscing about the golden era of the farm when she had first met Jack. Then it had been a thriving concern, populated by larger-than-life characters from the Victorian era, all long gone.

Jack also had plenty to say about his formative years but stopped short of talking about the war. I suppose that's understandable when you've seen your older brother's head blown off, just five feet away from you. I knew about this because Nellie told me one day when he was not around. Instead, we stuck to talking about childhood pranks, leading me to conclude kids had always been the same, despite the picture Edith liked to paint of children in her generation behaving impeccably. Jack had been quite a mischief-maker in his youth, it seemed.

We had a nice arrangement going regarding his evening newspaper. He loved the local rag but was finding the half-mile walk into the village to pick it up difficult these days, so I had been tasked with picking it up for him. It cost eight pence but he always gave me two ten-pence pieces, allowing me to spend the rest on sweets for my trouble.

That amount went a long way in 1981, being enough for a Curly Wurly or a packet of crisps. And I mean a proper full-sized Curly Wurly, not the diminutive modern version. Alternatively, I could get a decent selection of penny sweets, with the pink Shrimps being my favourite. I continued to fetch his paper after school when it restarted. By saving some of the extra cash, I was now able to buy a 7" single every week.

I hadn't seen as much of Martin and the others as usual during the holidays as they were already being funny with me now that they knew I was going to Wolfminster. But their treatment of me was nothing compared to the alienation which a new arrival at the school was to face as we moved into May.

Since my childhood, some events in the calendar have risen in stature whilst others have declined. Halloween, for example, is probably third only to Christmas and Easter now in terms of the merchandising frenzy that surrounds it. But May Day, much loved by children for generations, seems to pass almost unnoticed in the new century. This wasn't the case back in 1981.

The occasion was a big thing in our village, with a May Queen chosen by the primary school from the ten-plus age group who would be going up to secondary school in September. This year the girl selected was

Carey Evans, who I didn't care for. Even at the age of eleven, she acted like a diva, not that I had much to do with her. Girls and boys didn't mix much at that age and I had seen enough of Carey and her little crowd of hangers-on to know she was best kept at a distance.

On May Day morning, a horse-drawn carriage always transported the Queen to the village green. There, the children would entertain the villagers with traditional square dancing before taking to the maypole, twisting numerous coloured ribbons elaborately around the pole as they danced.

It wasn't a bank holiday, falling as it did this year on a Friday, but there was still a big turnout as everyone stopped what they were doing for an hour and came along.

Most of the shops in the village were locally owned, and the proprietors thought nothing of closing for an hour and coming down to the green. Retail was a different world back then. There was no evening or Sunday opening and the shopkeepers even gave themselves the afternoon off on Wednesday, known as early closing day, another quaint custom that seems to have fallen by the wayside.

It was a cool and cloudy day but thankfully the rain held off. I rather enjoyed the dancing, which we had spent all the previous week rehearsing. While I was performing I noticed that the bracelet was glowing red. I had no idea why. Was some accident about to befall me or one of the others? If so, it wasn't giving me any clues, and in the event nothing happened anyway. Everything went off without a hitch.

It was only when we got back to school late morning that I twigged what the bracelet was alerting me to. It was rare for outsiders to move to the village, even as late as 1981. The world was changing fast, away from our sleepy backwater, but here no one spoke differently or looked different to us. Almost every kid in our school could point to at least three generations of their family buried in the churchyard. So when someone from another culture did turn up, it drew attention.

Enter Maeve O'Brien, a recent arrival in the village and now starting at the school. Even before the teacher introduced her, everyone was staring at her. New starters at this age were practically unheard of, and she stood out right away. Her hair was vivid, a mass of red, cascading curls, and even this early in the year the spring sunshine had brought out a multitude of freckles. Her clothing marked her out as different right away; a lightweight, green linen dress adorned with intricate Celtic-inspired patterns.

"Everybody, I want you to say hello to Maeve who is joining us today," said Miss Bakewell, as we gathered in our corner pen for circle time just before lunch.

"Hello, Maeve," chorused the class half-heartedly, looking curiously at the nervous girl in the strange green dress.

"Hello," she said back, and with just that single word, spoken in her southern Irish accent, you could see the looks on the faces of many of the kids in the room. They were all thinking the same thing; *she's not one of us*.

I didn't stare at Maeve like they did. Instead, I focused on the reactions of the others, notably Carey, now back in her normal attire after her stint as the May Queen. Already I could see the look of contempt on her face as the bracelet pulsed furiously red on my arm. It wasn't just the girls, either. Martin generally only picked on other boys but I could see him too, a cruel look of relish on his face at the mileage he was going to get out of this.

Why was I taking such an interest in all this? Because I knew that four years from now, after incessant bullying from the prejudiced kids in the village, she would hang herself, unable to cope with the abuse any longer. It had dominated the news headlines at the time, being as it was a shocking and tragic end to a beautiful young life.

Nobody took the blame. She was depressed, said the papers, full of teenage angst, and had even been listening to The Smiths just before she died. Excuses, excuses. It was us who had killed her, everyone in that classroom, and I blamed myself as much as anybody else. We had thought it funny, from the Irish jokes, which were commonplace at the time, to doing impressions of her accent and calling her vile names.

I only knew her for a relatively short time as after the end of this term I had gone off to Wolfminster. She went on to St Jacob's and I never saw her again. The abuse continued there, eventually driving her to the depths of despair. And it had all begun here, today.

"Carey, there's a spare place on your table for lunch, why don't you show Maeve the ropes?" suggested Miss Bakewell, not realising that was about the worst thing she could have proposed. Even now, aged just eleven, Carey was well on the way to evolving into the uber-bitch she would ultimately become. I know this because I had the misfortune to run into her now and again during my teenage years, and each time she had grown progressively worse.

Since my table was next to Carey's at lunch, I tried to eavesdrop on as much of the conversation as I could. It wasn't easy in the crowded room. We didn't have a dedicated canteen so the open plan work area doubled up as our lunch space. The meals were brought up from the kitchens in metal trays and some of the older children were appointed as servers to dish out the food.

I can't say I cared for this arrangement. Having grown up around the farm with all our fresh produce, it's fair to say the quality at school was seriously lacking and some days practically inedible. To avoid eating the worst of the fodder, I had come up with some ingenious ways of disposing of it. It was amazing how much of the hard mashed potato one could adhere to the underside of a desk.

As for the revolting gruel called semolina, that was a little more challenging to dispose of. My way was via a small toffee tin I kept in my trouser pocket which could be surreptitiously filled up and then emptied down the sink later. If you didn't like something you only had to have a small amount so the tin was more than adequate.

Fridays, however, were good because it was always fish, chips, and beans. I was sitting next to Martin who had an annoying habit of trying to nick my chips, as well as playing stupid practical jokes such as unscrewing the lid of the vinegar bottle so some kid's meal would get swamped. Fortunately, I had long become wise to such tricks.

While Martin was blathering on about Aston Villa winning the league, I strained to see and hear what was going on at the next table. What I could make out was not pretty. It seemed that Martin wasn't the only one who liked to pinch people's chips.

Carey and her sycophantic sidekick Jane were sitting on either side of Maeve, systematically stealing the food from her plate. As they did this, they taunted her relentlessly.

"You're Irish so you don't need this food because you must be on hunger strike," said Carey.

"Yes," said Jane, grabbing a handful of chips from Maeve's plate. "Just like that Bobby Sands on the news. My dad says he's starving himself to death."

"But he's from Northern Ireland," protested Maeve. "I'm from Cork. Bobby Sands is British. He has more in common with you two than he has with me."

"You're all Irish and you're all terrorists," said Carey. "Look out, girls, she's probably got a bomb hidden under the table." And as she spoke, she cruelly yanked at Maeve's rich red hair.

Without exception, all the girls around the table laughed. I looked to see if there was a teacher in earshot but as expected there were none nearby. The girls weren't stupid. As soon as an adult appeared on the scene, they would all be sweetness and light. I thought Maeve had stated her position with clarity when explaining about Bobby Sands but it wasn't going to do her any good. My experience of this sort of situation was that it didn't matter how good the response you came up with to counter ignorant comments. The bullies smelt blood and they were going to get it, regardless of what you said or did.

I was unable to do anything from where I was. Children were not allowed to leave the table during the meal but I resolved there and then that I was going to help Maeve as soon as I could. She was going to need it because the abuse continued into the afternoon and not just from the girls.

After lunch, it was break time when I still played football out on the field with Philip and Martin, despite Martin's growing hostility towards me. I wanted to avoid them today in order to try to befriend Maeve instead. I knew this would raise eyebrows but quite honestly, I didn't care. I was leaving the school in a couple of months and if I could make life more bearable for her while I was still here, I would. I planned to give the others the slip on the way to the football field but as soon as we got outside Martin spotted Maeve and made a beeline for her.

"Hey, I know loads of Irish jokes," he said. "My grandad tells them all the time. Let's try a few out on that weirdo new girl."

"No, don't, Martin," I lamely began but he was already marching over towards her.

"Hey, Maeve," he said. "Why wasn't Jesus born in Ireland? Because God couldn't find three wise men or a virgin."

"Do you even know what a virgin is?" retorted Maeve, suggesting she was more worldly-wise than Martin, and gutsy with it. It was hard to imagine her reaching the depths of despair that would cause her to take her own life. But I suppose that even the strongest person can get worn down eventually if the abuse continues long enough.

Martin ignored her response and continued, "Did you hear about the winner of the Irish beauty contest? No, me neither."

It was time to intervene because I remembered a particularly nasty joke he had told a few days before about an Englishman, a Scotsman, and an Irishman, and I had no desire to hear it again, particularly not in Maeve's presence.

"Alright, Martin, that's enough. Leave her alone."

"Ooh, look at you! Why are you sticking up for her? Hey, listen to this everybody. Nick fancies Maeve!"

A small crowd had gathered around and now they began chanting, "Nick fancies Maeve, Nick fancies Maeve." It was incredibly childish but as I often had to keep reminding myself, we were children.

"No, I don't. I just think you're a bloody coward, picking on a girl."

"Oh, yeah? Would you rather I picked on you instead, then? Come on, big man, going off to your big posh new school soon, are you going to stick up for your new girlfriend?" And before I could answer, he punched me squarely in the jaw, knocking me to the ground. How many more times was I going to get a beating at the hands of Martin for the sake of the greater good?

I didn't bother getting up, much to his disappointment. No sense in getting hit again but I still got the obligatory kick in the ribs for good measure. At least he wasn't allowed to wear his DMs to school. He got away with it because, as usual, the teachers were conspicuous only by their absence.

"Come on, Philip, let's go and play footy. We'll leave this pansy here to play with his girlfriend." And off they went. But if I thought I was going to get any gratitude from Maeve, I was mistaken. By the time I got to my feet, she was on her way back inside. I started to follow, even though we were not supposed to go inside at lunchtime unless it was to go to the toilet. It turned out that was exactly where she was going, as I just caught a glimpse of the back of her red hair as the door to the girls' cloakroom closed behind her.

It was a sensible move, I suppose. Many was the time at Wolfminster I found my only sanctuary in a locked cubicle, and even then it wasn't safe if my tormentors figured out where I was. Then they would start lobbing balls of toilet paper soaked with water over the top, or even worse, those smelly yellow cubes from the urinals. But no one other than me had seen her go in so I was confident she would be safe for the moment. I headed back outside, wisely steering clear of the football field.

The rest of the day passed relatively incident-free, as I tried to keep an eye on her without coming across as a stalker. After lunch, I saw her making her way to the art room, so I followed and did some painting on the other side of the room while one of the teachers showed her how to use the pottery wheel. Carey and the others were nowhere to be seen. It seemed she had been given a temporary respite.

It struck me that I knew very little about her life. Why would I? I had made no effort to get to know her before. I had an uneasy feeling that I had been joining in and being just as bad as the rest of them. Kids could be extremely cruel, particularly in this era. You only had to look at the reaction to the recent appearance of Joey Deacon on *Blue Peter* to see that.

What had started as a well-meaning exercise to present those with disabilities in a positive light had backfired spectacularly, at least in our school. Deacon had cerebral palsy and far from showing sympathy, the day after the broadcast every kid in the school came in doing mocking impressions of him.

For years after that, I recall the name Joey being used as a term of abuse. I had forgotten all about this until I came back to 1981 but it was amazing how quickly it caught on. Such was the power of early 1980s television, when kids watched the same shows at the same time every week. If something notable happened, everyone was talking about it the next day. That simply didn't happen anymore in the era of streaming.

Try as I might, I couldn't muster up any further memories about Maeve. I had no idea what had brought her to the village but I was determined to find out and the bracelet was offering encouragement, giving me the green light in support.

She might have had a less stressful afternoon but home time would be another matter. Anything could happen once we were off the premises, when as far as the school was concerned, their responsibility was at an end. No parents came to pick us up at our age, and there was no security gate to be opened, just a wide-open driveway leading out of the car park with pavements along both sides. Security around the school was virtually non-existent because back then, just like the occupants of Meadowbrook Lane not locking their doors, no one deemed it necessary.

I dodged Martin and the others and made sure I left at the same time as Maeve, intending to try to strike up a conversation with her. But barely fifty yards from the school, Carey, Jane, and a couple of other girls were waiting for her around a corner.

"Oh, look who's here, it's the Paddy girl," said Carey, moving threateningly to block her path, fists clenched, leaving no doubt as to her intentions. And that's when I once again stepped in.

"Get out of the way, Carey," I demanded, stepping between the girls to create a space for Maeve to pass.

"Stay out of this, Nick," replied Carey. "Or maybe we should start calling you Mick."

This last statement brought peals of laughter from the other girls but I stood my ground.

"If you want to touch her, you'll have to come through me," I said, hoping she wouldn't call my bluff. Regardless of the outcome, fighting with girls was a big no-no. Thankfully, she did back down and grudgingly moved aside.

"Fine, take your little banshee home," said Carey. "But you won't be around to protect her all the time."

"I'm around now," I said, as Maeve walked through the gap without saying a word. As soon as she was clear, I followed, then after a few steps I heard one of Carey's gang wolf-whistle behind me.

"Ignore them," I said to Maeve, who quickened her pace. I wasn't sure if she was grateful or even welcomed my presence, but once we turned into the next street she stopped and turned to speak to me.

"Why are you doing this?" she asked in her beautiful, soft Irish lilt, looking genuinely puzzled as she spoke. "You're only making trouble for yourself, and besides I don't need help. I can look after myself."

"Because I know what it's like to feel like an outsider," I said. "Believe me, this village can be an incredibly hostile place if you don't belong."

"What makes you think you don't belong? How long have you lived here? All your life, I'm guessing. You must have because you've got the same accent as the others."

"Yes," I admitted, not sure how to elaborate. "I mean, I'm not an outsider yet, but I soon will be."

"How do you know?" she demanded, looking me squarely in the face for the first time, inquisitive green eyes probing into mine, trying to work out if I was genuine or not.

"It's not easy to explain," I said, glancing down at the bracelet and noting it was still green. I had been working to a strict rule that I should never tell anyone the truth about my situation but perhaps Maeve might be the person to change all that. Could I get her to trust me?

"No, I'm guessing not. You know there is something different about you, Nick, but I can't work out what. I'm not sure if that's a good or a bad thing."

"At least let me see you home," I said.

"That won't take long," she said, and it didn't. It transpired she only lived in the next street, in one of the village's older, quite spacious properties. How or why she had come to live there I did not know yet but now we had opened a dialogue it shouldn't be too difficult to find out. Keen to see her again, I took the plunge at her front door, trying not to come across as too nervous.

"Listen, Maeve, are you free tomorrow? I was thinking maybe we could meet up. I could show you around the village. I assume you've only recently arrived here?"

She looked at me quizzically, pursing her lips as she continued to try to weigh me up.

"I got here a few days ago," she said, as I heard a woman call from within her house, "Maeve, is that you?" Interestingly, it was in an English accent.

"OK, we'll meet up," said Maeve decisively. "You can call for me about eleven."

"It's a date," I said, instantly regretting my choice of words and backtracking. "I mean, no, not a date in the traditional sense of the word, just…"

"It's fine," she said, stepping through the door, and adding, "I'll see you tomorrow," before closing it behind her.

Fortunately, the school football team's season had finished at Easter so my Saturdays were now free. I was worried that we'd be hassled if we spent too much time in the main part of the village, so instead I took her for a walk down by the river, away from prying eyes. Once we were past the lock, we got into a good chat, telling each other about our lives. After a slightly awkward beginning, we soon discovered we had plenty in common, including a mutual interest in music.

"Who's your favourite band?" I asked as we wandered along in pleasant spring sunshine, watching butterflies fluttering amongst the wildflowers that thrived along the riverbank, and listening to the steady stream of birdsong all around us.

"The Undertones," she answered. She could hardly have made a better choice.

"I love The Undertones!" I exclaimed. "I've got one of their singles, 'Wednesday Week'. It was one of the first records I bought last year when I got my record player."

"My favourite song of theirs is 'My Perfect Cousin'. I had a copy of it in Ireland but had to leave it behind when we left." Suddenly, her voice was full of enthusiasm, now we had found some common ground.

"I've got a cousin who's far from perfect," I said, "but perhaps we'll talk about her later. How come you didn't bring your records with you?"

"That's another thing we ought to talk about later," she replied.

The sunshine faded and it began to rain so I brought her back home. Mum, as I had expected, was more than welcoming to a new friend visiting the house. She wasn't keen on me hanging out with Martin, given all the trouble over the years, so was probably pleased to see me finding some less dangerous company. She even offered Maeve a freshly made sausage roll, which was eagerly accepted. We went up to my room and spent the afternoon playing records and chatting.

The conversation was light-hearted to begin with, with her taking the piss out of my *Black Hole* wallpaper, but soon took a darker turn, as she explained how she had ended up in the village. Her mother was English and had grown up here but had married an Irish plumber whom she had met on holiday in Spain. She had moved away to Cork twelve years ago but had been forced to flee at short notice due to her husband's increasing alcoholism and domestic abuse. Now they were staying with Maeve's aunt who still lived here in the village.

Next, I told her all about my life, including my forthcoming move to Wolfminster, followed by the sordid story of Tracy and Dad. The longer we spoke, the more I knew I had to share the one thing that I simply couldn't keep to myself any longer. I needed to tell her what was coming and the only way I could do that was to tell her about the bracelet and my trip through time.

First I told her about Mum and the upcoming trip to New York. Then I explained why I had befriended her and what I knew about her future. It was a hell of a lot to lay on a person in one afternoon, particularly someone I had only just met, but the way I looked at it, I had nothing to lose.

She had no reason to believe a word of it but the jewel stayed green the whole time I was talking and she remained engaged throughout. It was the strangest thing, but I could sense the energy from the bracelet emanating from it as I spoke. Was this part of its power, to increase my powers of persuasion, so that when I needed to lend a helping hand, it would be accepted?

As a final piece of proof, I got her to touch the jewel. It might have been invisible, but it was still physically there and she marvelled at the solid touch of what was seemingly fresh air.

I held nothing back, ending with the shock revelation of her suicide, and then I stopped, leaving an uncomfortably long silence hanging in the air as I studied her pensive face and awaited her response.

"Well," she said finally, "the future looks bleak for both of us. Or rather it did."

"How do you mean?"

"I mean we both know what is to come now. And that means we can alter it. I'm sorry you've been burdened with all this on your own for so long but that's all over now."

"You're going to help me?" I asked, scarcely believing how well this had gone.

"Just you try and stop me. And we'll be helping each other. It'll be you and me against the world. Are you in?"

"What do you think?" I said with delight, as I realised she was right.

I wasn't on my own anymore.

June 1981

Life had improved considerably since Maeve and I had found each other – for both of us.

Somehow it didn't feel so bad to be an outsider when you had an ally in the same boat. I had heard Edith, never short of a proverb, spout the phrase "a trouble shared is a trouble halved," on many an occasion and for once the old battle-axe had a point. Together, Maeve and I felt ready to face anything.

Merely by associating myself with her, I had brought my upcoming alienation forward. Martin, Simon, and Philip still hung out with me for the moment but never missed an opportunity to rib me about both Maeve and Wolfminster. I was becoming the outsider of the group and wasn't sure how much longer we'd be playing together. I believe that it was down to jealousy when it came to Maeve. We were approaching the age where boys began to become more curious about girls and her wanting to hang out with me annoyed them.

As spring morphed into summer, I found myself outdoors a lot of the time. Now that I was getting older I was being asked to help on the farm at weekends but my evenings were mostly free. When the weather was good, I played out after tea, only coming home after dark.

My peer group went through a succession of crazes at this age. We would become obsessed with something for a short period before losing interest and moving on to something else. In June 1981, it was all about cricket, inspired by the start of The Ashes, and England's charismatic Ian 'Beefy' Botham.

After we had all watched coverage of the first test on television, Simon suggested we should have a game. That meant Martin going home to get his cricket bat, something I had reservations about due to a vague memory from the past about being whacked with the thing. I checked the bracelet but it wasn't issuing any warnings, so I decided to risk it. If Martin started turning nasty, I would just remove myself from the situation.

In the end, it wasn't him I had to worry about but grumpy old Stan, the man with the outside toilet, who lived in the middle of the five cottages. He truly was a miserable bastard of epic proportions. Generally there was a decent community spirit in the lane, but he and his wife Edna were the exceptions. They rarely interacted with the other adults but had made their dislike of children crystal clear. Even riding my Grifter past their house was enough to generate a rebuke, with Stan coming to the door in his string vest to bellow things like, "Bloody kids! This isn't a racetrack!"

After a while we began answering back, particularly Martin, who had nothing to lose because Stan didn't know where he lived. It was different in my case, and on the rare occasion when Stan did speak to my parents it was usually because he was coming up to our cottage to complain.

Thankfully, they paid lip service to his rantings most of the time. They knew just as well as I did what a cantankerous old beggar he was. After he had vented for a bit they would say that they would have a word with me and then shut the door on him as quickly as they could, because on top of his lovely personality, he also stank – a heady mix of overcooked cabbage, sweat, and urine.

Mum said that it wasn't just an inside toilet they lacked, but any sort of bathroom facilities at all. Brenda claimed that all they had was an old tin bath in the living room that they used once a week. I found it hard to believe that was still the case as late as 1981, and the information had come from the suspect source of Brenda, but if it were true, it would explain a lot. How she found out, I don't know, because Stan and Edna never invited people in. Perhaps she got her kicks from peering through the window when he was having his bath.

Our cricket match was a rather makeshift affair. Other than Martin's bat we had no other proper equipment, so had to improvise. We decided to play in the lane but the gravel base was rock hard, which rendered pushing stumps into it an impossibility. Besides, we did not have any.

Instead, we used some bricks from a pile that had been lying in the farmyard for years, left over from a barn that was built before I was born. We stacked these up on top of each other at opposite ends and found a manky old tennis ball that looked as if it had been chewed by one of the many stray dogs that roamed around the village.

We didn't have to worry about obstructing the lane with the bricks because by 7pm everyone was home and there wouldn't be any cars coming along. We set it all up between Wisteria and Sunflower and then got into a lengthy discussion about the scoring system, which almost descended into an argument.

Bearing in mind that Martin was the one holding the bat, and that none of this was of any importance, I wisely acquiesced to his suggestions. It was agreed that a six would be hitting it all the way to the junction with the main road at the end of the lane, whereas we nominated several places that would be deemed a four, including landing it in Stan's front garden which was, quite frankly, asking for trouble.

The first one to knock it in there was Martin, right into a bunch of lupins, sending petals scattering everywhere. Simon, who was fielding, nervously nipped over the low wall and retrieved the ball, seemingly undetected by Honeysuckle's fearsome occupant.

Philip was less fortunate. His ball whacked the front window, thankfully not breaking it. It was a good job we weren't using a proper cricket ball because that would surely have shattered the glass. Within a couple of seconds, the door was flung open and a fiery Stan emerged, purple-faced, sweaty and panting, with veins that looked as if they were about to pop out of his forehead. I've no idea what he had been doing but the front of his string vest was wet and covered in yellow stains.

"Look out!" shouted Martin. "It's Old Gitface!"

"You bloody little shits," bellowed Stan. "I'll have you this time, you see if I don't!"

We scattered up the lane towards the farmhouse, knowing he would never catch us, but that wasn't his intention. When he got to our homemade stumps, he grabbed the bricks, one by one, and began hurling them up the lane towards us. One narrowly missed striking Simon on the back of his head. What Stan was doing was potentially lethal but we didn't think about that at the time, and seemingly nor did anyone else.

It was another example of changing times because if a grown man started hurling bricks at a group of small boys in the 2020s, someone would call the police and he would be hauled off. But back then, as far as the rest of the lane's residents were concerned, it was just Stan being Stan and nobody had been hurt so it didn't matter. At least he put on a good show for Brenda who had a grandstand view from Sunflower, nose poking eagerly through the blinds.

After that night, I resisted any further suggestions to play cricket. In any case, I had other things on my mind. Maeve and I had discussed several times what I ought to do about Dad and Tracy, and on the last weekend of June, a few days after the cricket debacle, an opportunity finally arose.

With the extra work I had been doing on the farm, I now had plenty of money so in addition to buying a single every week, was also able to save for the occasional album. That was true of Maeve as well. She had managed to bag a paper round despite being below the required age to have one. The man who ran the paper shop was so desperate for kids who wouldn't rob him blind of sweets or dump the papers in the river that he would take a chance on anyone. The only thing you had to do when he asked you how old you were was say "thirteen," and you were in.

On Saturdays we went down to Harman's together to buy our records, and since Maeve didn't have anything to play hers on, we always went straight back to mine to listen. This week, I picked up 'Ghost Town' by The Specials, and she bought 'Will You' by Hazel O'Connor. But when we got home, Mum had some unwelcome news.

"Hello, you two!" she said enthusiastically, as we walked into the kitchen clutching our precious vinyl. "You're just in time to try a couple of my scones."

That bit wasn't the unwelcome news as my mother made delicious scones. She made delicious everything, and we watched now as she removed them from a baking tray and placed them on a wire rack. I could almost taste the moist, crumbly pastry, generously laden with fruit, as the smell of them assailed my nostrils.

"Thank you, Mrs Taylor," said Maeve, in the polite way that kids always speak to every parent other than their own. And now, came the bad news.

"Dad and I are going out for a meal again tonight," she said. "I was going to ask Julia to babysit but Tracy popped in earlier and offered to do it. She said she loved looking after you last time and is really looking forward to doing it again."

"I bet she is," muttered Maeve under her breath, just softly enough for my mother not to hear.

"What's the occasion?" I asked. I didn't think it was anyone's birthday.

"Oh, there's a few of us on the carnival planning committee going. We've been working hard getting everything ready for the past couple of months so we thought, why not treat ourselves to an evening out?"

The carnival was a big thing in our village. It took place on the first Sunday of July and was an event that virtually everyone turned out for, except for the odd misery guts like Stan. The rest of the village enthusiastically joined in, festooning their houses with bunting, and dressing up for the parade. My mother was a keen participant, taking the opportunity to exhibit her art each year at a stall on the field. She had also been one of the organisers for many years.

"Right," I said, not sure what to say at the prospect of another evening under Tracy's supervision. I reached for one of the scones, but Mum tapped me on the hand to discourage me.

"Give them a couple of minutes to cool down," she said. "Then they'll be perfect."

After a few minutes of idle chit-chat, we each had a scone, and then went upstairs to listen to our records, where Maeve was most insistent about what my next move should be.

"Your mother has no idea why Tracy's so keen to babysit," she said. "But this could be the opportunity you've been waiting for."

"To do what?" I asked.

"To expose what's going on. You said that last time your dad walked Tracy home they got up to stuff outside. If she's that keen to babysit, it's obvious she's hoping for a repeat performance. All you've got to do is get your mum out there to catch them in the act."

"What good will that do?" I asked, baulking at the prospect of what the revelation would do to my mother.

"Because if she knows, surely she'll throw him out," explained Maeve. "That's going to leave her with sole responsibility for you. She's hardly going to jet off to New York under those circumstances, is she?"

"If only that were true," I lamented. "But I live in a lane with two grandparents, two aunts, and two uncles. There's no shortage of people to look after me. Mum would just arrange for me to stay with one of them for a few days. Probably Edith, which would mean starvation rations for a few days. Also, I reckon with Dad out of the picture, she would be even more determined to go to New York and make a success of her life, just to show him what he threw away."

"All valid points," said Maeve. "But I still think you need to expose him sooner rather than later. Think about what happened before. The family fell apart and Tracy ended up with everything in the end."

"Only because Mum died. If she hadn't, Tracy would never have got her hands on this place. It belongs to my mum's side of the family, not my dad's."

"Precisely. This means you've got to get the truth out in the open now, regardless of what happens afterwards. Show everyone in the family what a scheming cow Tracy is. They'll never accept her back into the fold after that."

I pondered what she was saying. One thing I had to say for Maeve, despite her tender age she had a solid grasp of how adult relationships worked. A mature head on young shoulders, as Edith would no doubt say. Perhaps that was why we got on so well but something in her choice of words concerned me.

"You're talking as if Mum might still die," I replied.

"And she still might. Lord knows, we'll do everything we can to prevent it but you've got to consider the possibility that if she's determined to get on that plane you may not be able to stop her."

"I will find a way," I insisted, looking to my wrist for guidance, and gaining reassurance from seeing the jewel pulsing green in agreement. "I've got the bracelet, remember? It will help me when the time comes. It has before."

"Either way, you've got to expose the affair and you'll never get a better chance than tonight. I know it will be painful for your mother but it's got to be done. Get this part sorted now and we'll worry about the rest of it later. One problem at a time."

She was right, and the bracelet agreed. Tonight it was, then. All I needed to do was find a way of getting Mum to see the two of them together.

The evening followed a similar pattern to before. Tracy turned up dressed like a tart, and as soon as my parents were out of the door made herself at home on the sofa, drink in one hand and cigarette in the other.

I had no desire whatsoever for any repeat of our conflict last time so stayed out of the way upstairs where I played records until after it got dark. This wasn't until about ten since we had only recently passed the summer solstice. While I was there, I weighed up my options.

The priority was to remove Tracy from my life permanently, even if it meant losing my father in the process. It seemed harsh to come to that conclusion but he had brought it on himself.

When they got home, things happened broadly as they had done the previous time. Mum and Dad were both merry again, more so than on their anniversary. I put that down to being among friends which always encourages the drink to flow. After a bit of small talk, Dad predictably offered to escort Tracy home, and my mother readily agreed. I had been hiding upstairs on the landing but as soon as they were out the front door, I came bounding down the stairs, fully dressed, and in my Dunlop Green Flash trainers, much to Mum's surprise.

"Nick!" she exclaimed cheerfully, buoyed by the evening's refreshments. "It's nearly midnight. I thought you'd be in bed by now. Why aren't you in your pyjamas?"

I got straight to the point. "You need to follow them."

"Whatever for? It's only three doors down, I'm sure they know the way."

"Exactly, so why does he need to go? And how long do you think he'll be? A couple of minutes? Or will it be more like twenty?"

"Nick darling, I don't know what you're implying," she said, but I noticed her brow furrow slightly and her smile drop. Was this the first doubt filtering into her mind that something untoward might be going on?

"Oh, you do, Mother. Don't be blind to it. Go after them and see for yourself. Catch them in the act."

"I will not," she said, her anger growing, not at him but at me. "He's my husband and I trust him. And you shouldn't even be talking about such things at your age. Who's been filling your head with this nonsense? Is it Maeve? You do spend a lot of time with her and I've heard about what happened between her mother and father."

The bracelet was glowing red suggesting that I wasn't going about this the right way. If I didn't get a shift on, the window of opportunity was going to pass.

"If you won't go, I will," I shouted, sprinting past her and out the front door, figuring she'd have no choice but to follow. I was only dressed in jeans and a T-shirt but unlike the last time, that was more than sufficient. It was a warm night.

"Nick! Come back here at once!" she shouted, following me through the doorway, just as I had hoped. That was the first stage of the plan accomplished. Now I just had to hope I could get her to where she needed to be without alerting my quarry to our presence.

I ran down the lane, past Sunflower, which was in darkness. Poor old Brenda. If she had stayed up she could have been treated to a real show tonight. I slowed down as I approached Honeysuckle, scanning ahead in the darkness but I couldn't see them. My mother was following me and called out my name again. That wasn't ideal. She might alert them, wherever they were. Visibility improved as I approached Fuchsia as William had left the outside light on again but unlike last time, they weren't up against the side of the cottage. So where had they gone?

I heard them before I saw them. The field opposite the cottages beyond the brook was part of the farm and full of rapidly growing corn at this time of the year. The moans I could hear coming from behind the hedge that bordered the field could only mean one thing. I stopped, turned around, and waited for my mother to catch up figuring that if she could see me standing there she would have no further need to call out.

As she approached I saw her open her mouth, ready to administer an admonishment, but before she could speak, I put my fingers to my lips and whispered, as loudly as I dared, "Listen!"

She stopped and then, even in the semi-darkness, I saw the realisation cross her face as she heard them at it. I couldn't believe they were being so brazen as sound did carry out here and most of the cottages had their windows open at night in the summer. Perhaps they thought that everyone would be asleep by now, or that it was just teenagers messing about and would ignore it. Technically, they would be half right, because one of them was a teenager. They just didn't know that the other was a forty-two-year-old man.

Either that or the two of them were so consumed by lust that they didn't care. People could be remarkably lax under such circumstances, and in this case, they were going to suffer the consequences of their carelessness.

"Go back inside, Nick," said my mother in a low voice. "I don't want you to see this."

"It's OK, Mum. I already know about them. I've seen them before. That's why I had to get you out here. I'll wait here. Go and catch them."

"Go and call for William and Jackie then," she said. "I want them to see this too."

She walked a little further along to where a bridge over the brook led into the field, then disappeared behind the hedge. Meanwhile, I did as she suggested and went over to knock on William's door.

"Young Nick," he exclaimed, answering in his dark red pyjamas. "What brings you here? Is Tracy alright?"

"At the moment, but she might not be in a minute," I answered, just as we heard all hell break loose on the other side of the hedge where my mother had just caught them with their pants down.

"What the fuck do you think you're doing?" I heard her shout out, as no doubt did the rest of the lane.

"What's going on, William?" asked Jackie, who had come down in her nightdress.

"Some sort of commotion in the field," he answered, as Mum emerged over the bridge, roughly manhandling a half-dressed Tracy in front of her. Shortly afterwards, my father followed, clad only in his shirt and underpants. They were lit up by the light from the bedroom windows of Rosemary where Edith and Dennis had been woken up. Doubtless, they would be getting a bird's eye view of all of this. Goodness knows what Edith would make of it with her notoriously puritanical views.

"Get off me, you bitch," shouted Tracy, who was looking rather bedraggled. She still had her skirt on but I suspect it was minus her knickers, and her top was ripped where my mother had grabbed hold of her, leaving one of her breasts practically hanging out.

"No chance, missy," said Mum, who could be mightily tough when she chose to. That's what an upbringing on a farm with all that physical labour did for you. She propelled the weaker girl in front of her, right up to the front door where she shoved her, sending her sprawling onto the doorstep to land in a heap on the floor right in front of her parents.

"Mary, whatever is going on?" asked Jackie, as my father nervously approached behind us. I would have

137

thought it was blatantly obvious but for the benefit of all present, my mother spelled it out in precise Anglo-Saxon terms.

"I've just caught this little slag fucking my husband in the cornfield," she replied, shocking even me. I had never heard my mother swear before tonight and now she had dropped the F-bomb twice in a couple of minutes. The word loses its shock value from people who utter it constantly but when it comes from an unexpected source it packs a real punch.

"Oh, Tracy," said Jackie, looking down at her daughter who was lolling about on the floor, and beginning to laugh drunkenly. She must have made a sizeable dent in our drinks tray again this evening.

"So what if I was? About time someone had some fun around here. Look at you all, nothing but a bunch of dried-up old farts. That was probably the first decent fuck anyone's had in Meadowbrook for years."

"Tracy, stop it," said Jackie, crimson with embarrassment. "Come inside at once."

"She's not coming in here tonight," said William, as Dad sheepishly stopped, about twenty feet away. "She's not coming in here ever. If Tony wants her, he can have her, but not here," he added, giving my father a disgusted look.

Good old William. I knew he would stick up for Mum. When it came down to it, the Cartwright blood was thicker than water.

"I agree," said Mum. "You can both get out of here, tonight."

"But where will we go?" asked Dad pathetically. And to think, all these years I had blamed Tracy for taking him away from me. The truth was, he was just as guilty as she was.

"Anywhere away from here," said my mother. "We don't want you anymore."

"That goes for me too," said Edith, who had come out to see what all the commotion was about. "In all my years of living in Meadowbrook Lane, I've never seen such wanton wickedness. May God have mercy on your two souls is all I can say."

They were outnumbered and they knew it. Tracy, suddenly realising the seriousness of the situation, dropped the act and turned to her mother, who was the only one who hadn't yet publicly disowned her.

"You aren't going to let them do this to me, are you, Mum?"

"I think it's best that you go for now. I'll pack you a bag," she said, disappearing upstairs.

"Same goes for you," said Mum, turning to Dad who was still standing behind us, lost for words. What could he possibly say?

"Are you going to be alright, Mary?" asked Edith, with genuine concern.

"I'll be fine. Come on, Nick, we're going home. I'll pack you a bag, Tony, even though it's more than you deserve. Then, don't come back here again. Ever."

She took my hand and we began to walk up the lane, as the bracelet glowed green on my arm. It thought I had done the right thing and so did I. My mother had proved remarkably resilient, given the circumstances, and I was as happy as I could be, all things considered, at how things had turned out.

Barely ten minutes later I watched from the window as my father and cousin got into the Marina and drove away for the last time. I felt no sorrow. This had been the right thing to do – at least for now.

Then I heard my mother sobbing in her room. She had been strong in the face of adversity but the pain was overwhelming her now.

July 1981

If there was one thing my family was good at it was rallying around. After the scandal had broken, there was barely a waking hour when one of my mother's siblings wasn't in the kitchen, drinking tea, and offering a shoulder to cry on.

A healthy dose of sympathy was bestowed in my direction as well. This included an unwelcome extra-large hug and kiss from Carol when she made a rare trip from her ivory tower on Boars Hill to lend her support. The prevailing view was that I must be traumatised by what had happened, but if anything it was the complete opposite. I was overjoyed at the changes I had wrought.

Before, when Tracy and Dad's affair came out, it still caused a scandal, make no mistake about that. However, the altered circumstances led to a very different outcome. They had been able to dupe the family into believing they had been thrown together in grief after Mum's death. Playing the sympathy card, my father had been able to move her in, ultimately leading to them inheriting the house in the will when my grandparents passed on.

Most, including Jack and Nellie, had grudgingly accepted their relationship in the end, but William never had. He was disgusted with both my father and his daughter and never spoke to either again, eventually abandoning the farm and moving away from the village. If he had been that angry then, it was hard to imagine the level of outrage he must be feeling now.

Dad and Tracy didn't have a leg to stand on this time. They were universally condemned by everyone in the family, as well as by the community at large. They managed to find accommodation at a local guest house in the short term but it seemed unlikely that they had much of a future in the village. They had even been barred from the local pub.

My attention now turned to Sunday, and the carnival at which Mum would first meet the art dealer who would offer to whisk her off to New York. With a few days to go, Maeve and I met up at my house after school to talk about the implications.

"It seems to me that all we need to do is stop her meeting this American fella, and then she'll never go to New York," ventured Maeve.

"That's one option," I replied. "But I'm not sure if it's the best one. Mum's been devoted to her art all her life, and always talking about getting that elusive big break. From what I remember of this guy he was the real deal. What he was proposing had the potential to completely change her life."

"Oh, it did that alright. Changed it from alive to dead."

"Unintentionally," I said. "My ideal scenario would be to allow them to still meet, and then ensure she takes a different flight when the time comes."

"Is that worth the risk?" added Maeve. "It sounds like you're sailing unnecessarily close to the wind. What if you can't stop her?"

"I've been wrestling with that dilemma ever since I got here," I said. "But whenever I've thought about preventing them from meeting, the bracelet has given me the red warning light. It doesn't think I should intervene, at least not on that front. The truth is, I don't think I could stop them meeting even if I wanted to. Mum's still having the stall on Saturday, despite everything that's happened. I overheard her talking with Edith last night. She's determined to hold her head up high in public."

"What about this dealer? What do you know about him?"

"Not a lot. I remember that he was middle-aged and dressed like an old fashioned gent, waistcoat, hat, that sort of thing. Oh, and his name was Art. I couldn't remember that at first but it popped into my head the other day."

"You're joking!" exclaimed Maeve. "Art the art dealer. What are the odds?"

"Indeed. But that's all I know. I can't remember his surname, and even if we could spot him in the crowd, how would we prevent him from walking past Mum's stall?"

"I still think you're playing with fire, allowing them to meet, whatever the bracelet says."

"Maybe I am but I don't see any alternative. She's not going to give up the stall and we can't stop him coming to the carnival. Our best bet is to be around when they meet to gather as much information as we can."

Plans in place, we looked forward to the village's annual day of celebration. It began early as the local children waited excitedly outside their house for the Balloon Man to arrive. He was an elderly gent who dressed up and rode a colourfully decorated bicycle around the village every year, giving out balloons and sweets to the kids. It doesn't sound that exciting but when I was a small child, the anticipation of his annual arrival was second only to that of Father Christmas.

At lunchtime, there was a parade and a traditional race around the streets, where grown men would push each other in prams and drink a pint at every pub on the route. After that the festivities moved to the playing field, where there would be various events, displays, stalls, and a funfair.

The stalls were a mixed bunch. Some were taken by local businesses advertising their wares, others by organisations such as the scouts, who used it as a recruitment opportunity. Then there were the charity stalls like the tombola, where punters bought a raffle ticket, and won a prize if they got a number ending in zero or five.

Many of the prizes were donated by the villagers and some were rather dubious. Among the cans of beer and bottles of pretend Champagne that was in reality a brand of sparkling cider called Pomagne, there would also be dodgy tins of food that had been gathering dust in the back of cupboards for years. I stopped participating after the year I won a tin of Smedley's peas.

Finally, there were the small, individual stallholders, selling their homemade jam or arts and crafts. It was one of these that my mother took each year to showcase her paintings.

She normally did quite well, selling several at around ten pounds apiece, though she didn't make any profit from it. Considering the amount of time she spent crafting them and the cost of materials, including the frames, she was probably making a loss. But she wasn't in it just for money. She got a wonderful sense of fulfilment from knowing that people loved her paintings enough to want to display them in their homes.

Today would be the day she was going to get the recognition she deserved. Unfortunately, I had not been there to witness this previously, and neither had my father. I had been with my friends at the funfair, riding bumper cars and daring each other to go on The Cage, a new and scary ride.

While we were doing that, Dad had been with many of the other men in the beer tent. But he wasn't there this time. I saw neither sight nor sound of him nor Tracy all day, suggesting they had decided to stay away. This was probably a wise move, as given the mood of the villagers, he might well have been lynched had he shown his face around a crowd of tanked-up locals.

I wanted to know exactly what I was dealing with when Art the art dealer came along so I forewent the pleasures of the funfair, offering to help Mum on the stall. She was more than grateful, having been noticeably clingy towards me since Dad's departure. With him out of the picture, and Linda seemingly washing her hands of us, I was suddenly all she had left.

It was a sunny day, which always brought out the crowds, and the atmosphere was as lively as ever. Our brightly coloured stall, festooned with ribbons and balloons, was one of dozens filling the field. As I helped Mum arrange some of her paintings on a trestle table, I was assailed by the smell of burgers and fried onions wafting our way from one of the many food outlets dotted around. Music from an old-fashioned hurdy-gurdy was playing not far away, and children were running around everywhere, squealing with excitement, many of them still in costume from participating in the parade.

It was an idyllic scene, a world away from the violence that was erupting a couple of hundred miles away in Toxteth this same weekend. It was the second big outbreak of rioting this year, following the Brixton disturbances in the spring, but you would never imagine such a thing happening here in our affluent, cosy Oxfordshire village.

"Are you sure you're happy staying here with me, Nick?" asked my mother. "Wouldn't you rather be with your friends at the fair?"

"I don't mind helping," I said, not that there was much to do. Groups of people were wandering past, stopping to look appreciatively at the paintings, some of them making complimentary remarks. We hadn't made any sales yet, though. At every opportunity, I scoured the crowds to try to spot the mysterious Art but there was no sign. I felt confident I would recognise him if I saw him, even though I had only seen him once when he had come to the house, forty years ago. He had a very distinctive look.

Maeve turned up in the traditional Irish dress she had been wearing the day I first met her, with her red hair neatly tied up in a bun. She was carrying two ice-creams with flakes in them.

"Here, I've brought you a treat!" she said, handing one to me. "Sorry, Mrs Taylor, I probably should have got you one too."

"That's very thoughtful of you, Maeve. And you can call me Mary. I've gone off the name Taylor. I'm thinking of changing it back to Cartwright."

As she spoke, an elegant young woman in a floral dress stopped to look at a painting of the Old Mill, as it had looked before Martin had caused the roof to cave in. While she was distracted, I turned to Maeve.

"Any luck?" I asked. She had also been combing the field, looking for the elusive Art.

"No one that fitted your description. I saw Carey, though. She called me a whore."

"She's lovely, isn't she?" I said sarcastically. "I guess we had better stay here, then."

It proved to be a long wait, though at least we had a decent view of the arena from the stall. From our vantage point, we were able to watch the tug of war, the donkey derby, and the falconry display. Then, just as the sun began to sink towards the horse chestnut trees at the bottom of the field, our man showed up.

Business had been slow. We had only sold four paintings all afternoon, leading Mum to ponder why. It was the worst year since she had started having the stall. I believe I knew the reason but didn't say anything.

My theory was that people were staying away because of her marriage break-up. They knew all about what had happened, sympathised with her, and therein lay the problem. There was an elephant in the room, or to be pedantic, the field, and they simply didn't know what to say to her. So this year, rather than stop, have a chat, and maybe buy something, they walked on by rather than risk an awkward conversation.

It was getting late when Art made his entrance. Mum was dealing with an elderly lady who used to work as a dinner lady at our school before she retired. She was admiring a painting of a nearby old stone bridge that spanned the Thames.

"This is lovely," she said. "Reminds me of when I was a girl. We used to jump off that bridge in the summer. But I couldn't afford ten pounds. I'm an old-age pensioner. I could give you five pounds for it."

"Go on, then, Mrs Walters, as it's you. But don't tell everyone."

"You're selling yourself short there, lady," said Art loudly, in a broad American accent which immediately commanded attention. He had appeared seemingly from nowhere and was now standing next to Mrs Walters, admiring the paintings.

Then he declared, "I'll give you a hundred pounds for the lot."

The new arrival stood out in a field where most of the men were dressed in shorts and t-shirts. His attire harked back to an era when men took greater pride in their appearance. Despite the warm day, he did not seem overly bothered by the heat, though he was wearing a well-tailored cream suit, red bow tie, and waistcoat. His middle-aged features, with impressive sideburns, and a Panama hat to match his suit, exuded the image of a sophisticated, old-school gentleman.

"And you are…?" asked Mum.

"Of course, how rude of me. Art's the name. Art Kensington. Art's the name and art's my game," he added. From anyone else, this would have come across as incredibly cheesy but somehow he carried it off with aplomb.

"I'd still be selling myself short," replied my mother. "I've got fifteen or sixteen paintings left here."

"Please, Mrs…" said Art, pausing to allow her to introduce herself.

"Cartwright," she said firmly. "And as of today, it's Ms, not Mrs."

"Please, Ms Cartwright, you misunderstand. When I said a hundred pounds I meant per painting."

"What?" she said, in a stunned voice. "But that's…that's fifteen hundred pounds."

"Well he's not having this one," said Mrs Walters, grabbing the painting she had already laid claim to, and handing my mother five grubby pound notes she had already pulled out of her purse. "You said I could have this one."

"And so you can," said Art, pulling out a weather-beaten brown leather wallet. I could see that it was practically busting at the seams with the amount of currency crammed into it. "Now how about I buy it off you for a hundred pounds right now, Mrs Walters? Not a bad mark-up, don't you think?"

"Oh my," said Mrs Walters, her eyes widening as he peeled off five twenty-pound notes. It was probably more money than she had handled in her whole life. "Yes, please."

She took the money and scurried off, scarcely able to believe her luck as Art studied the painting. "My, my, you've captured the essence of this bridge splendidly.

This is exactly the sort of stuff I'm looking for to display in my Olde England exhibition at my gallery in New York. American art lovers are going nuts over this sort of thing right now. I'll take these and any others you may have. Do we have a deal?"

This was my chance, and I seized it before she could reply.

"On one condition," I stipulated. "That you do not try and get her to go to New York to help you sell them."

"Nick!" exclaimed my mother, angry at my interruption. "How dare you be so rude?" She turned back to Art and added, "I'm so sorry. We've had a rather difficult time in the family this past week and my son has taken it rather badly."

"No, I haven't," I protested. "I just don't want you going to New York. I need you here."

"Listen, young buddy, why don't you take your friend here to the fair for a bit, while me and your mother talk business," he said, peeling another twenty-pound note from his wallet and offering it to me. "My treat."

But I didn't reach out for it.

"I don't want to go to the fair, Mum," I protested. "I want to stay here and protect you."

"I don't need protecting, Nick. Now do as you're told and go to the fair. And thank this kind man for being so generous."

I had no option but to back down. Art wasn't doing anything wrong, after all. Why would Mum think she needed protecting? Grudgingly, I took the money, and Maeve and I went and spent it on rides, sweets, and the arcade. Twenty pounds went a long way but I couldn't fully enjoy myself. I had let an opportunity slip by.

The following day, Art visited the house to discuss their deal but I was unable to disrupt proceedings because he came while I was at school. When I did get home, my mother was excitedly waiting for me, clasping something in her hand.

"Nick, come and look at this!" she exclaimed, before eagerly thrusting a cheque for £5,000 under my nose. "Do you realise what this means?"

"I do," I replied but I felt I wasn't thinking about the same thing that she was.

"I was worried about how I was going to make ends meet with your father gone but not anymore. With this money, I can divorce him and we won't have to worry. We don't own this house. We rent it off your grandparents for a nominal sum, so I don't even have to pay him off. I know it's hard for you but we'll get by. Everything is going to be alright."

"Promise me you won't go to New York, then. I assume he asked you?"

"He did. He's planning a big exhibition of my work at his gallery next month, and he wants me to officially open it. I can't not go. I've dreamt of this moment all my life."

"It could end your life," I said, unsure of how to explain further. How could I get her to understand?

"How, exactly?" she said.

"In a plane crash!" I exclaimed, committing myself. "I've been having nightmares about it. The jet you're travelling on will crash into the Atlantic, with everyone aboard killed. That's why you can't go."

"Those are just bad dreams, darling. I can't not go just based on that. I realise that you're fearful. Your father's gone and now I'm going away for a while. Understandably, that would be unsettling for you."

I was fighting a losing battle. She thought these were just irrational childhood fears and that she was reassuring me, the way any mother would with her child. What could I say to convince her otherwise?

"I can tell you the precise date the plane crash will happen. August 3rd. If you absolutely must go, just don't go on that date. Any other day you'll be fine."

"OK, Nick," she said. "I will tell Art I can't fly on that date if it makes you feel better."

I could tell from the tone of her voice she wasn't taking this seriously. She was just trying to calm me down. All I could do for now was accept what she had said and leave it at that. Encouragingly, for the next few weeks, there was no further mention of New York.

There was great excitement in the lane towards the end of July as the country geared up for a royal wedding. The future King Charles III was to marry his so-called sweetheart, Lady Diana Spencer, in a fairy-tale ceremony. That was the way the media painted it. I knew otherwise but kept that to myself as Edith, Jackie and the others eagerly prepared for a street party.

They claimed it would be as big as the one we'd had for the Queen's Silver Jubilee, which truly had been an occasion to remember. By coincidence, it was also my birthday, which meant a double celebration, not that I was in any mood to celebrate given the situation.

Along with some early birthday cards, an official-looking brown envelope arrived the previous morning addressed to Mrs Mary Taylor. When she opened it in front of me, she was thrilled at receiving her first-ever passport, though did comment that she should have officially changed her name to Cartwright.

When I quizzed her about why she had applied for it, she said she had been thinking of spending some of the money from the paintings on a foreign holiday for the two of us. I didn't buy it. Art must have suggested she get one because she had never shown any interest in going abroad before.

Maeve showed up early on the big day, bringing me two birthday presents which were current chart records by Depeche Mode and Kirsty MacColl. I opened them at the same time as the present from my mother, a ZX81 computer, complete with a Boots own brand cassette recorder. The Sinclair machine was laughably primitive compared to modern standards with its tiny 1K memory, but at the time it was considered state of the art, and every kid wanted one. The opening of these presents was the one bright spot in what was to prove a dismal day.

Edith had decreed that the whole family would watch the wedding in the farmhouse, gathered around Jack and Nellie's 20" Ferguson television set. This was intended to evoke memories of the Coronation when Jack's father, who was the patriarch of the family at the time, had just become the first owner of a television set in Meadowbrook Lane.

The coverage started early with the ceremony due to take place late morning. It felt eerie watching it, knowing the wedding was a sham and the fate that would later befall the princess. Of course, my assembled family hadn't a clue about any of that. All they saw was the romance of the occasion, with frequent "ooh, aah," and "doesn't she look lovely," remarks.

By lunchtime we were all out in the lane, with fizzy drinks for the kids and booze for the adults. The nation had been granted an extra bank holiday so nobody was working, not even William who had got up at the crack of dawn to do what was necessary on the farm before taking the rest of the day off.

Everyone was there, including Stan and Edna putting in an extremely rare appearance, even though they were the only ones who hadn't put any form of bunting out in front of their house. Simon and I wisely stayed out of their way, following the recent cricket debacle. Sadly there was no Maeve, as she had gone back to a party in her street, which was a shame as I could have done with her support with what was to unfold.

All was going well until Art drove into the lane in a vintage Bentley, parking up behind Stan's old banger outside Honeysuckle.

"Who's this?" asked Simon as we quaffed Lilt, a rare treat, at one of the trestle tables that had been set up along the lane.

"Trouble," I said as I watched Art, full of enthusiasm, coming towards us clutching an envelope in his hands.

"Art, how wonderful of you to drop by," said Mum.

"I'm not interrupting, am I?" asked Art, ever the gentleman. "I don't want to crash you good folks' party."

"Of course not, you'll be more than welcome!" said Mum. "Come and meet everybody. Dennis, get this man a drink."

The new arrival was swiftly surrounded by the residents, eager to find out who this mysterious and wealthy stranger might be. Brenda, as expected, was right at the front of the queue, along with her daughter Karen. For the next few minutes it was all introductions and exchanges of pleasantries, but I knew he had come with a purpose. I stayed close by, keen to hear what he had to say and intervene if necessary. The bracelet approved, giving me the green light, but was it going to be much help when it came to the crunch? It wasn't offering any hints as to what I should do next.

Eventually Art managed to get my mother's undivided attention, and then we got to the business end of the proceedings.

"Mary, do tell me, did you manage to get yourself a passport, as per my suggestion?" asked Art.

So it was Mary now, was it? What happened to Ms Cartwright?

"I did indeed. It arrived this morning."

"Excellent, my dear, because I am flying back to the States tomorrow. Your paintings have been successfully shipped to the gallery, and are being prepared for the exhibition as we speak. And I would like you to fly to New York next week, first class of course, to open it as my guest of honour. Here's your ticket."

He handed over the envelope, as the surrounding neighbours who had been hanging on his every word burst into a spontaneous round of applause.

"When next week?" I demanded loudly, as my mother opened the envelope.

"Oh, um…it's the 3rd," she said, perusing the ticket. "That's Monday."

"No, Mum, you cannot go on that date," I shouted at the top of my voice. "You promised."

I turned to Art, and added, "She can't go on Monday. Any day but that."

"Yes, but all the arrangements have been made," he began to explain before Edith intervened.

"How dare you be so rude to your mother! And to our guest, you ungrateful little wretch. Mary, he's been an absolute terror since Tony left."

"He needs taking in hand," added Dennis ominously.

"He's a menace to the neighbourhood," grunted Stan, sticking his unwelcome oar in. They were the first words I had heard him utter all day.

"Please, Mum, you cannot go on that plane." Clutching at straws, I turned to Nellie, and said, "Gran, please, read her tea leaves and tell her not to go."

"I did them the other day and there's nothing to worry about," said Nellie. Of course there wasn't. She made it all up, I don't know why I had even bothered to ask. It had been a stupid thing to say but that's what happened when people were desperate. And I was most certainly that right now.

"No, you cannot go," I screamed, trying to snatch the envelope out of her hand, intending to rip up the ticket. Before I could, I felt a strong pair of arms grabbing at me.

"That's quite enough of that, my lad," said Dennis, manhandling me roughly away. "I've got a good mind to take my belt to you. Now, I'm taking you home where you can stay in your room. We don't want you down here any longer, spoiling things."

I could smell the scotch on his breath as the scruffy old git pushed me roughly up the lane.

"She's not going!" I shouted. "I'll stop you."

But would I? Not with the mess I'd made of it so far. As for Dennis, I resented him dragging me by my t-shirt so I wriggled out of his grasp and ran back up to the house without looking back. I might not have been able to destroy the ticket but I still had one other option.

Back at the house I headed straight for the kitchen drawer where all the important documents were kept, and began rummaging through, looking for her new passport. Nothing. Where would she have put it? I ran upstairs to her room to continue my search, and after a couple of minutes, I discovered it in the drawer of her bedside table. All I needed to do was destroy it and then all this would be over. She'd never have time to get another one before Monday.

And then, I heard the creaky stair go. Someone was coming up. I raced out of the room, passport in hand, just as Dennis reached the top of the stairs.

"What have you got there?" he demanded with a look of fury on his face. "Give that to me!"

"What are you doing here?" I said, genuinely fearful. I knew that Dennis had a violent streak in him, because Simon told me that he had once beaten him to within an inch of his life after he and Martin had been caught stealing sweets from the post office. And the half bottle or so of whisky he had polished off already this afternoon was surely going to make matters worse.

"I'm here to teach you a lesson. One you'll never forget. Your father's not here to discipline you anymore so that responsibility falls to me."

My fears were confirmed. I couldn't escape him because there was nowhere to go. And he was big and I was small. I backed slowly away into my bedroom, terrified at what was to come. He followed, looking around the room disapprovingly.

"When I think of all the effort I went to, decorating this room in *Star Wars* wallpaper for you. And this is the thanks we get."

"It's *The Black Hole*, you stupid old twat. You and your skinflint of a wife couldn't even get that right, could you?"

I didn't care anymore. I had already resigned myself to the beating that was coming so I figured I might as well be hung for a sheep as a lamb. Another phrase I had heard Edith spout many a time.

He shoved me down onto the bed, pulled down my pants and smacked me hard, several times on the bottom. Then he stopped.

"Let that be a lesson to you, young man. And next time, I really will take my belt to you."

Then, mercifully, he left, leaving me sobbing. I wasn't just crying from the pain of the punishment he had inflicted, even though it stung like fuck. My real misery stemmed from my total failure to achieve what I had set out to do. What's more, he had taken the passport with him. If I hadn't acted so rashly, I could have destroyed it at my leisure.

I looked down at the bracelet in desperate hope of some guidance, but there was nothing, not even a flicker. I just lay there for what felt like hours, in despair and pain. I couldn't remember ever feeling so low.

Worst birthday ever.

August 1981

I had pleaded and I had wept. I had even tried telling her the truth about the life I'd led before and the principal reason I had come back in time to 1981.

All of it was to no avail. Mum simply didn't believe me and nor did anyone else in the family. I hadn't tried to convince them personally but they had all heard my outburst at the party, and none of them had spoken in my support either then or since. All I had was Maeve but she couldn't help me any more than I could help myself.

The more I brought the subject up at home, the more irritated Mum became. To make matters worse, she didn't keep our conversations to herself. She was so concerned about my obsessive behaviour that she confided in other members of the family. They just made things worse, coming out with patronising twaddle about me "just going through a phase" and other similar remarks that filled me with rage and frustration.

On Sunday lunchtime, the day before she was due to depart, they held a family meeting in our kitchen. Edith and Dennis were there, along with William and Jackie. I pretended I was going to Maeve's but snuck back in through the rear door and up the stairs. Our staircase took a ninety-degree turn halfway up so I positioned myself just far enough around the bend to be out of sight.

Here I could listen to the conversation below, and what I heard made for grim listening. I had heard Edith say in the past that eavesdroppers never hear anything good about themselves and this was a prime example.

They discussed the practicalities of my mother's trip first, with William confirming that he would give her a lift to Heathrow. It wasn't long, though, before the conversation rolled around to me. The problem child.

"I wish I could be more excited about this trip but I'm so worried about Nick," stated Mum. "He desperately doesn't want me to go. He's convinced that the plane is going to go down and I'm going to be killed."

"It's understandable," said Jackie, who was probably the most sympathetic of the group towards me. "He's lost his dad and now you're going away. It's a lot for a boy of that age to deal with."

"Then he needs to grow up a bit!" said Dennis. "When I was his age there was a war on. We didn't have namby-pamby parents pandering to us like they do to some of these spoilt brats nowadays. We just got on with it. The lad just needs discipline, that's all. Spare the rod and spoil the child."

"He'll get plenty of discipline with us while you're away, don't you worry, Mary," added Edith.

I didn't like the sound of that. It had been decided, not by me I hasten to add, that I was going to be staying at Edith's house while Mum was away, sharing a room with Simon. The idea filled me with dread.

"I don't want you getting heavy-handed with him, Dennis, do you understand?" said Mum. "I'm still cross with you over last time. There was no need for that. Now you are not to hit him, do you hear me? He's been through a very difficult time."

"I don't see why he can't stay with us," said William. "We've got a spare room now Tracy's gone. It seems silly him squeezing in with you."

"I want him with us," insisted Edith. "You'll be too soft on him. They need keeping a close eye on at that age. I don't like some of the children he spends his time with either. That Maeve's got the devil in her, I'm sure of it."

That was an unjustified slur which I could only assume was prejudice against her because she was Irish. Edith was no better than the kids at school, and she hadn't finished banging on yet.

"Nick will be much better off in a good Christian house. I said as much to the vicar this morning after Sunday service and he agreed. He suggested that he might find salvation by joining the Pathfinders. They've helped many a troubled young person to find the light."

"He is not a troubled young person," insisted Mum. "He's just upset because I'm going away. That's why he's made up this story about the plane crash to deter me. And remember, I'm only going to be away a week. When I get home, everything will be fine. You'll see."

"Well, I still think he needs a strong hand," said Dennis.

And so it went on and on, for a good hour or more. After they had all gone, I made one final attempt to persuade her but it was fruitless, as I knew it would be. That left me with only one option: sabotage.

I couldn't destroy her ticket or passport because I didn't know where they were, having searched the house from top to bottom for them without success. I had shown my hand too early by trying to dispose of her passport before, and now the family were keeping them safely out of my way. I guessed that they had been given to one of the siblings for safekeeping.

With less than a day to go, my options were running out. I'd had all year to figure this out, yet here I was, still no nearer to a solution.

In an ideal world, I'd have prevented the aircraft from taking off at all. There were over two hundred souls on board, all of whom were going to perish when it went down. I had wondered many times if I had been going about this the wrong way. Why was I going to all this effort to stop my mum from getting on board a doomed flight? Would it not be better for all concerned to stop the thing taking off in the first place?

Easier said than done. How did an eleven-year-old stop an international flight? According to the bracelet, he didn't, because it wasn't giving any indication that preventing or delaying the flight was the solution. It made me wonder what the point of the thing was in the first place. Keith had claimed it was meant to put things right in the timeline, and what fitted that brief better than saving hundreds of lives?

The bracelet only helped when it felt like it. I had made good use of it plenty of times but by now I was seriously questioning the thing's motives. It called the shots over what should or shouldn't be done here in the past, not me, and it didn't seem to follow any moral or logical pattern. For every person it helped, it ignored another.

It certainly didn't seem to care about all those people who were going to a watery grave in the Atlantic tomorrow. They would all be other people's mothers, fathers, sons, and daughters. What about their feelings and their losses? Weren't they important? If only the damned thing could communicate properly, I might be able to get some answers to these questions. But all it had to offer most of the time were the green and red flashing lights, frequently without any context.

I toyed with one idea after another. At one point I thought about phoning through a terrorist threat, claiming there was a bomb on the plane. But the bracelet rejected that idea with a red signal as soon as it popped into my head. It wasn't a very realistic course of action anyway. I hadn't a clue what number to call. I didn't know if there was any such thing as a terrorist hotline in 1981 and even if there was, at the age of eleven I had a high-pitched voice that was unlikely to be very convincing. Doubtless, the authorities were used to kids making prank calls. I speak from experience.

It was a common thing back then, given the combination of phone boxes and troublemaking kids out on the streets. I had seen it first-hand a few weeks before when we had been down in the village one afternoon after school.

Martin, on a whim, had nipped into the phone box outside the post office, and dialled 999. He proceeded to ask for the fire brigade, promptly telling them that the school was on fire. This was, in my opinion, a bloody stupid thing to do as it could have diverted them from a real fire. Mr Jones was furious when the fire engine turned up, sirens ablaze, and gave the whole school a massive bollocking about it at assembly the following day, knowing the culprit was likely to be in the room.

All things considered, preventing the plane from departing was beyond my capabilities. It was going to take off whatever I did. My only option left was to ensure Mum was not on it. If she didn't get to the airport in time, she would miss the flight. It was as simple as that.

She could still go to New York; she would just have to get a later flight or go the next day. It would be no skin off Art's nose to pay for another ticket with the amount of money he had. It would just be an inconvenience, that was all.

I lacked the strength to physically prevent her from leaving, so I focused instead on her mode of transport. If William's car wouldn't start, he wouldn't be able to take her to the airport.

She needed to check in for her flight no later than half past nine. During the discussion in the kitchen, they had agreed to leave at seven in the morning, figuring that ought to give them ample time, even accounting for the rush-hour traffic. It would also allow William time to milk the cows before they left. The farm only had three, a declining herd that was a fraction of what it was in the farm's heyday, but it was still a task that needed to be carried out each morning.

Whatever I was going to do, it had to be enough to delay them for an hour or more at least, given the slack they had built into their schedule. I had several ideas about how to incapacitate the car and in the end, I decided to try a combination of things. The timing was crucial. Whatever I did, I needed to ensure that they weren't aware of it until it was too late.

I had identified three targets which were the petrol tank, the battery, and the tyres, in that order. If possible,

I wanted to avoid doing any permanent damage to the car. All I needed to do was to stop it from moving for an hour or two that morning.

I didn't want to invite any further suspicion, so on Sunday evening I acted as if I had finally accepted the situation. I had a long and tearful farewell with my mother, and they were not crocodile tears by any means. Her safety was far from assured and if I messed tomorrow up, this really would be goodbye. The only comfort I could draw was from the bracelet, which kept assuring me I was doing the right thing. But I remained distrustful of it.

One part it did disapprove of was my idea of tampering with the fuel tank. Initially, I had planned to siphon out the fuel. I had once seen Dennis do this when he had sold his old Ford Anglia. It had been done at Edith's insistence, as she had not wanted to give away half a tank of two-star petrol to the new owner. It was an easy enough thing to do with cars of this era, unlike later cars which had valves to prevent the practice. But the bracelet advised against it.

It also repudiated my idea of pouring sugar in the tank. I had seen this done in a film but had no idea if it worked in real life or how much would be needed. I doubted that the half bag we had spare in the cupboard would be enough, so in the end I concluded that tampering with the petrol tank was a foolhardy idea. I didn't want to do anything that might make the car potentially dangerous while my mother was inside it, and messing about with a highly flammable liquid fell into that category.

That left the battery and the tyres. There was plenty I could do with them but it was vital William didn't discover my sabotage until he came to start the car in the morning. My plans required the cover of darkness so I went to bed dutifully, like a good little boy. Then I waited until my mother retired, just about ten, bearing in mind her early start in the morning. I left it another couple of hours to ensure everyone else in the lane would be asleep and then crept downstairs.

My target was William's eight-year-old orange Datsun Cherry, which was parked at the side of Fuchsia Like most of the car owners in the lane, he never bothered to lock it and usually left the keys in the ignition. That sounds like asking for trouble but car theft in our village was unheard of. I believe it went on in some of the rougher parts of Oxford but I never heard of a single vehicle being appropriated where we lived. And even if the city's finest thieves and joyriders did somehow find their way to our quiet part of the world, I highly doubted they would be interested in the Datsun.

Of course, I could have just taken the keys and thrown them in the brook but if I did that, they would have ample time to make other arrangements. Besides, for all I knew, he might keep a spare set in the house.

The first job was to flatten the battery which was an easy task. All I needed to do was switch a few things on and it would quickly drain down. I turned the key far enough to activate the electrics without starting the car, then turned on the radio, with the volume low. I also flicked on the lights, but only the sidelights. It would take longer but I couldn't risk putting the headlights on in case they were seen from the bedroom window of one of the cottages. Finally, I switched on the internal light. An hour or two with all that lot running ought to do the trick.

I snuck back to the house to grab a couple of hours of sleep but that was all. I had a clock radio alarm which I set for 4 o'clock so I could go back to the car and see how it was getting on. By the time I got there, the lights had dimmed, indicating that the battery was drained, so I switched everything back off. As an extra measure, I lifted the hood and disconnected the terminals, adding a further problem to be dealt with. Then I went home to my bedroom and waited because I had only carried out half of the plan so far.

The next bit was trickier. It was all about timing. I knew that William would be getting up soon to milk the cows and I didn't want there to be any visual damage to the car. That's why I had left the tyres intact until now. I was also aware that Mum was planning to be up at six to give her an hour to get ready. This left me only a short window to do what needed to be done.

It was already light outside as I watched from the window for William to pass on his way to the farm, which he duly did around twenty-five to six. He had told Mum he would have done everything he needed to on the farm before seven, at which point he would call in for her on the way back. Hopefully, this meant I would be able to carry out the next phase of the plan undetected.

Originally, I had planned to hammer nails into the tyres, putting the car completely out of action. The bracelet hadn't approved, which made sense when I thought about it. If they saw the tyres had been destroyed it would be the same issue as if I had hidden the keys.

They would instantly seek alternative transport. Instead, I decided to let the tyres down in the hope they would waste time pumping them up. In preparation for this plan, I had already been up to the barn where I knew the pump was kept, to hide it, adding a further delay.

With all the tyres flat, I made it back to Wisteria just before Mum rose, unaware of how much of the night I had spent outside. I pretended I had just woken up and that all was well, enjoying breakfast with her. Then, around ten to seven, I started playing up again, begging her for one last time not to go. After much wailing and gnashing of teeth from me, a biblical phrase that Edith was fond of, I delivered my pièce de resistance.

"If you go, I'll run away! I swear I will. I'm not staying with Uncle Dennis. He'll hit me with his belt, I know he will. He does it to Simon all the time, he told me."

I clenched my fists in front of my face as I said all this and shook them to give the impression of a boy who was quaking with fear.

"Please, Nick, why are you making this so difficult for me? Dennis won't hurt you, he's promised me."

"A fat lot of good that'll do me as soon as you're out of the country. Now, please, for the last time, I beg you, do not get on that plane."

"Oh, Nick," she said despairingly.

"Right then, I'm off. Don't say I didn't warn you," I shouted, bounding out into the hall and through the front door, ignoring her pleas to come back.

I ran down the lane towards the bridge across which Tracy and my father had gone the night they had been caught with their pants down. As soon as I was on the other side, I ducked behind the hedge and made my way back along the other side of the brook. This was an ideal place to hide out as there were spots with small gaps in the hedge from which I could observe what was going on beyond, with little chance of being spotted. It was just like being Brenda but from the other side of the lane.

William, on his way back down from the farm, had been confronted by my mother who had rushed outside as soon as she had seen him approaching, her face etched with distress, which he immediately picked up on.

"Mary, whatever's the matter?"

"It's Nick!" she wailed. "He's run away!" As I watched I could see the streaks on her face where the tears had been running, which made me feel awfully guilty. I hated making her unhappy like this and had to remind myself that it was all for the greater good.

"What do you mean?" asked William. "As in, he's packed a bag and left?" He must not have seen me running down the lane. I had got away just in time.

"No, he took off just now, saying he was running away. He's desperate to stop me from going to New York. Maybe he thinks I won't go if he's missing."

"Mary, you cannot let this stop you going. You've said many times that this is the opportunity you've been waiting for all your life. Nick will be fine."

"Will he?"

"Yes. I don't think he's really run away. I think this is a last desperate attempt to stop you. He'll be back. Remember what Edith always says? They always come back when they're hungry. Now don't you worry about him. Jackie and I will take care of him. And I won't let Dennis harm him, you have my word on that."

"Thank you," she said, taking a huge gulp of air to calm herself down and try to stop the sobbing. "It's just making this so hard for me."

"Have you got all your things?" he asked. "We need to get going."

"It's all in the hall," she replied, leading him back in. A minute or two later they emerged, laden down with her luggage.

I was bathed in early morning sunshine as I crept stealthily along the hedge, taking up my new surveillance position opposite Fuchsia, eager to gauge their reactions when they saw what I had done to the car.

"I don't believe this!" exploded William, who doted on his little Datsun Cherry rather more than it deserved. "Someone's let all my tyres down!"

"Who would do a thing like that?" asked my mother, which I thought was obvious. It certainly was to William.

"Nick, obviously! I'm sorry, Mary, I've been sympathetic up until now, but this is going too far. I didn't want to say this but Jackie and Edith were talking last night and they are convinced that there is something wrong with him. I didn't agree at the time but now I've seen this, I'm not so sure. They think he should see a psychiatrist."

Now that his beloved car had been got at, William's support for me had evaporated. Perhaps I was destined to feel the sting of Dennis's belt after all.

"I don't want to talk about this now," Mum insisted. "We'll discuss it when I get back from New York but don't you go doing anything while I'm away. Right now, let's concentrate on getting to the airport. We've still plenty of time. Have you got a pump?"

"I've got a foot pump but it's up in the barn. I'll have to go and fetch it. Why don't you go in and have a cup of tea with Jackie? She's normally up by now."

The fetching of the pump took longer than expected thanks to me concealing it between two straw bales. By the time William returned and reflated the tyres the best part of an hour had passed, but now they were all set to go. Or so they thought until he turned the key and got no response.

"Bloody hell," said William, thumping the steering wheel in frustration. "Now what?"

He lifted up the bonnet to investigate, as Mum sat in the passenger seat, window down and arm outside, tapping her fingers on the door with increasing impatience as the minutes ticked away. It didn't take William long to figure out what was wrong. He reconnected the battery and got back inside but when he tried to start it again, he still had no joy.

"For fuck's sake!" I heard him exclaim at the pathetically slow whirring of an ignition that was never going to spark.

"Pull the choke out," suggested Mum.

"That won't help!" he said. "It's as flat as a pancake."

"We can't waste any more time," she said. "I've got to leave – right now."

"Maybe we can jump-start it. Shame it's facing the wrong way. Go and see if Dennis can help. He's got a set of leads."

She went to look but was soon back.

"No good. I just saw the back of his car disappearing up the lane. He's got some big decorating job on in Witney this week and said yesterday he would be leaving early."

"If we get Edith, Simon, and Jackie to help, we might be able to push start it down the lane," he suggested.

"Don't bother. Even if we do get it working, what else might Nick have done to it? I need to find alternative transport and fast. What about Stan? Would he help?"

"You must be joking. He wouldn't give you the steam off his piss. And besides, that old Morris of his is a death trap. It'd be lucky to get as far as Oxford, never mind Heathrow. There's only one thing for it. You'll have to get a taxi. Wait here while I call Rick."

He went back inside to ring Rick's Wheels, the only taxi firm in the village. Rick had a reputation for being unreliable, and as Mum waited, she became increasingly nervous at the escalating race against time, pacing up and down beside the stricken Datsun. By now, Edith had come out but wasn't offering much in the way of constructive help.

"How many times have I told you, Mary? It's the early bird that catches the worm."

"We've been out here since seven," Mum protested. "We were not to know the car would be out of action."

"Yes, and we all know why, don't we? I'm sorry, but that boy needs sorting out."

"I've already told William, you leave him alone until I get back. I mean it, Edith. If Dennis lays one hand on my son he'll have me to answer to."

"I still say we should have push-started it," said William, scanning the horizon for any sign of the unpredictable Rick who had promised to come right away but was nowhere to be seen. Finally, a good half hour after calling him, a green Vauxhall Cavalier hove into view.

"At last!" he exclaimed. I looked at my watch to see it was now a quarter to nine. Had I done enough?

Rick pulled up, and William hurriedly explained the urgency of the situation.

"Don't worry, Mrs Taylor, I will get you there on time," said Rick, who had bleached blonde hair and an earring in a dubious attempt to look like a pop star despite being nearly fifty. "Jump in."

"Cartwright!" she insisted, as she hopped in the back while William threw her luggage in the boot and slammed it shut. Rick floored the accelerator and the car screamed off down the lane as if he were taking part in the RAC rally, screeching tyres sending gravel flying everywhere.

She was gone, and all I could do now was wait. But where? I knew I would be in serious hot water as soon as I showed my face in the lane but I couldn't put it off forever. I decided I would stay away for a couple of hours to give William time to cool off, and then go back at lunchtime. At least Dennis wouldn't be around if he was working in Witney.

I went round to Maeve's, filled her in on developments, and then we watched TV for a little while. Daytime television was almost non-existent in the early 1980s but they did make the effort to put a few programmes on for kids during the school holidays so we watched *Cheggers Plays Pop* and *Why Don't You…?* After that, coverage of the latest Ashes test came on, which was of no interest to Maeve. At this point, we followed the advice of the theme tune of *Why Don't You…?* We switched off the television set and went outside.

By midday, it was time to face the music. I reluctantly made my way back home, taking Maeve with me for moral support, hoping Edith wouldn't say anything horrible to her after her comments the previous day. To avoid having to go past Rosemary, we cut through the fields and made our way down via the farmyard. But as soon as my home came into view, my heart sank.

There was a police car outside. Specifically, Bill Tanner's police car, which was a pale blue and white Austin Allegro with a blue light on top. I would have found this comical had the stakes not been so high. This wasn't a moment for levity.

Bill was our local copper. He had a police house in the village, knew everyone, and dealt with all matters in our small parish. That was the way things were done in rural backwaters in this era.

"What are the police doing here?" asked Maeve, as we rounded the corner.

"I'm not sure," I replied with trepidation. The first time around, all those years ago, it had been Bill who had come to break the grim confirmation of my mother's death. The moment was indelibly etched on my mind but he couldn't have come about that. It was too early. He had come in the evening before. The plane would have taken off by now but it hadn't gone down until mid-afternoon when it had been a few hours out from London. So what was he doing here?

As I watched him talking to Edith, Jackie and William, plus Brenda who had come out to see what was happening, I concluded, erroneously it turned out, that they had reported me missing and he had come to help find me.

I soon realised that was not the case. As we approached I could hear Edith wailing and see an ashen look on William's face. As soon as they saw me, Jackie ran over and wrapped her arms around me. Whatever was going on, it was serious.

"Oh, Nick, I'm so sorry," said Jackie.

"What's happened?"

"It's your…it's your mother," she said, leading me over to the others. She was barely able to get her words out and when I looked her in the eyes her lip wobbled and she burst into tears.

"Please, someone, tell me what is going on!" I demanded as they all looked at me, seemingly lost for words. Finally, Bill clarified the situation.

"The taxi taking your mother to the airport crashed on the A40, just outside Oxford. She's been badly injured."

"And it's all your fault!" screamed Edith, turning on me with a red face and a wide-open mouth screaming at me with every ounce of venom she could muster. "You truly are the devil's child!"

"That's quite enough of that, Edith," snapped Bill, with an authority that made it clear she was to shut up. Thankfully, she complied.

"Is she going to die?" I asked.

"I'm sorry, Nick, we don't know any more at this stage," said Bill. He was a kind man, aged around fifty, and a real old-fashioned type of community policeman. He was the sort who would help old ladies across the road or turn up at school to help teach kids the Green Cross Code. He always offered advice in a practical and friendly way without ever sounding patronising or bossy.

"No! This can't be happening," I screamed, overwhelmed with anger at the situation. Then I looked at the bracelet which was glowing green at me and felt filled with hatred at the cursed thing. A force for the good? What good had it done me? I wanted rid of the thing and I wanted rid of it now. Irrational and overcome by emotion, I ran away up the lane, ignoring the calls behind me to stop, even those from Maeve.

I headed for the barn where William kept his tools and grabbed the nearest thing I could find, a pair of old shears, to try to hack the thing off. This was ridiculous as I would have to hold the shears with both hands, rendering it impossible. That's how distraught I was. I wasn't thinking straight.

Next, I grabbed an axe and toyed with the idea of hacking at it, which was feasible but also incredibly dangerous. I might very well remove the bracelet that way but would probably take my arm off with it. Then I spotted a hacksaw on the bench and decided to try to saw it off. This was also insanity. One slip, and I could slash my wrist.

That was when William ran in, saw what I was doing, and unable to see the bracelet, jumped to the conclusion I was trying to kill myself. I dropped the saw and he dragged me away. I feared punishment but none was forthcoming. He just gave me a tight hug and reassured me that everything was going to be all right. I'm so glad it was him that found me, and not Dennis.

Before he grabbed me I had managed to get the hacksaw onto the bracelet but it hadn't made so much as a scratch on it. Whatever it was made of it was impervious. We were welded together, for better or worse, until this year was over, and I just had to accept it. Quite honestly, I didn't have the energy to fight it anymore anyway. The stress of recent days had exhausted me and there was nothing more I could do.

William led me outside and back to Fuchsia, where he and Jackie looked after me, allowing Maeve to come in at my request. They knew she was my best friend and that I would draw comfort from her presence. Thankfully, Edith was gone, driven by Bill up to the John Radcliffe where both Mum and Rick had been taken after the accident. We didn't know anything more other than that she was in a serious condition, and thus began a long afternoon of waiting.

Edith had promised to call when she knew more, and the afternoon dragged like an eternity as we waited for news. To try to lighten the mood, Jackie put on the radio, tuning into Radio Oxford so that Maeve and I could listen to Timmy Mallett's afternoon show for kids. Then, the hourly news bulletin came on.

"Reports are coming in that a passenger jet, flying from Heathrow to New York, has crashed in the Atlantic Ocean, about two hundred miles off the American East Coast. Initial reports suggest…"

That was as much of the story as we heard because Jackie exclaimed, "Oh my God, you were right, Nick! Did you hear that, William? That must be the plane Mary would have been on!"

And then the phone rang. William listened intently as Edith gave him the news from the hospital, which he happily relayed to us.

"She's going to be OK," he said, relief oozing from his every pore. "She had a heck of a bump on the head which knocked her unconscious, lots of cuts and bruises, a broken arm, and a couple of broken ribs. But that's all. And Rick's going to be alright too. Though Bill told Edith that he was over the drink-driving limit. Knowing him he'd probably been partying all weekend."

"Do you realise what this means, Nick?" said Maeve. "You did it. You saved her. Just like you said you would."

Jackie and William could only look at me in awe.

"It looks like Nellie's not the only clairvoyant in the family," said Jackie. "I'm so sorry, we should have listened to you."

"You had no reason to," I said. "I mean, I'm only a kid. No one takes any notice of a kid. But I am sorry about all the trouble I caused. And about your car, Uncle William."

"Think nothing of it," he said. "There's no long-lasting damage. The most important thing is that your mother is safe. And that's down to you, Nick. You're a hero!"

And then the tears came in deep sobs, emotion welling up inside me as the enormity of everything I had been through these past few weeks overwhelmed me.

"It's OK, Nick," said Maeve softly, as she took my hand. "It's all over now."

September 1981

For a few weeks, I was able to relax and enjoy the rest of the summer. The growing sense of helplessness that had gnawed at me as the flight date loomed was finally swept aside, replaced by a newfound sense of calm.

After that eventful day, there was a notable shift in the family's attitude towards me. The most dramatic change was in Edith. She had previously been convinced there was something wrong with me, even going so far as to suggest I might be possessed by satanic forces. Now she had done a complete about-face, hailing my prophetic warning about the ill-fated flight as a divine blessing. That I hadn't averted the tragedy, thus sparing only one life instead of hundreds, she conveniently overlooked.

Nellie had a different explanation.

"You see!" she pronounced as the family gathered to celebrate my mother's homecoming from hospital. "He's got the gift! It's been passed down in our family for generations. I had it, and now he has it too."

There was an obvious flaw in this proclamation, namely that hardly any of Nellie's predictions ever came true. If she had the gift, how come she had failed to realise the danger her daughter had been in?

I'm sure I wasn't the only person who realised this but nobody had the heart to point it out. Nellie's fondness for tea leaves and other astrological musings brought her great joy in her twilight years, and who would begrudge an elderly woman such harmless entertainment?

After six days in the hospital, Mum had returned home in good spirits, fully aware that she was fortunate to be alive. With her arm encased in plaster, painting was off the agenda for a while, and she was still in considerable pain from her ribs. In the medium term, she was expected to make a complete recovery.

We had already shared a tearful reunion during a midweek hospital visit. She had been full of contrition, apologising profusely for not listening to me before. This gave me the chance to explain all about the bracelet and how I had come back in time to save her. I even let her touch it, just as Maeve had. Then, I recounted all the things I had achieved since my arrival in January. She listened intently, hanging on every word, and expressing approval at the things I had done, though she did say she wished I had told her about Dad and Tracy earlier.

When I finished, I stressed how important it was that this went no further. The family had already come up with their own theories about my gift anyway, so at the welcome home party we indulged Edith and Nellie. If this was what they wanted to believe, that was fine by us. Brenda, who had once again managed to invite herself, spent a fair deal of time sniffing around suspiciously trying to find out more, but she didn't get anywhere. My secret was going to stay safely between Mum, Maeve, and me.

With lazy August days at hand, Maeve and I were able to make the most of our time, going out into the country, having picnics, and on wet days listening to music. I had no desire to hang out with Martin and the others anymore, which wasn't an issue as they never called for me anyway. It was probably the most enjoyable part of my whole year but in no time at all September rolled around, a month that would take Maeve and me in different directions.

My only responsibilities during this time were to the home, where due to her incapacitation, I had been helping Mum out with shopping and cooking, with Edith and Jackie also lending a hand. She finally made it to New York at the beginning of September, with my complete blessing this time. Although her arm was still in plaster, she was able to fly with assistance, and the exhibition, which Art had delayed for a month, was a great success. Back home, I had other things on my mind while she was away, my attention now focused on matters of schooling.

Part of me regretted deciding to take up the place at Wolfminster after I'd had a chance to get out of it. I had made that decision before meeting Maeve and I didn't like the idea of her being left to fend for herself at St Jacob's. I voiced my concerns as we lounged at her place on the evening before she started the new term, with the Top 40 providing the soundtrack to our conversation.

She had saved up money from her paper round to buy a twin cassette player with radio, and Sunday nights were a rare treat. It was the only time of the week that Radio One was able to broadcast in FM stereo, taking over the frequency ordinarily occupied by Radio Two.

"You don't have to worry about me," she insisted. "Whatever they throw at me, I'll handle it."

"That's what you probably thought before, and look at what happened. You're going to be on your own and there are a lot more kids at that school than the old one. Over a thousand, from all the little villages around here.

Chances are they'll be even more small-minded than the ones you've already encountered."

Maeve looked pensive, as the record playing, 'Japanese Boy' by Aneka, which had dropped down to number two in the chart came to an end. Then Tony Blackburn began the countdown, after trying to create some excitement and an air of mystery about what the new number one might be, even though everyone already knew. The charts were five days old by the time this show was broadcast, and we had already seen Soft Cell performing the new chart-topper, 'Tainted Love', on *Top of the Pops* on Thursday night.

"Yes, but I didn't have you, then," she replied, after a thoughtful pause.

"But I'm not going to be there. I'll be at Wolfminster."

"Doesn't matter," she said. "I have you as a friend outside of school, and even when you're not around, I'm under no illusions about what to expect. I'll be well prepared for it, and whatever they say, it'll be water off a duck's back. You know what they say, sticks and stones may break my bones, but words will never hurt me."

"You sound like Edith when you come out with phrases like that!" I remarked. "But what if they do use sticks and stones? Some of my friends do – quite literally. Earlier this year, down at the Old Mill, we were lobbing chunks of brick at each other."

"Have you seen anything of Martin and the others recently?" she asked.

"Not a sausage," I said. "They've disowned me. Just like they did before when it got close to the time I started at Wolfminster. But I don't think I've seen the last of them. You're not the only one who's going to have to look out for sticks and stones. I'm in for a tough time, and not just here in the village. At the new school too."

"When is it you start, again?"

"Not until a week on Monday. The terms at Wolfminster are shorter than at St Jacob's."

"I suppose that's one advantage," she said.

"Hardly," I replied. "They compensate by making us go in on Saturdays, remember?"

"You know, I still find that unbelievable," she replied. "It's like something out of Victorian times."

"That's an apt observation because the whole place is stuck in the nineteenth century. Saturdays are going to be rubbish now – no more *Tiswas*, and no more trips to Harman's afterwards to buy our records."

"We can go when you go back. They don't close until half five."

"I suppose so," I said, without enthusiasm. "School on Saturday. What a joke. Why the bloody hell am I putting myself through all this again?"

I had a strong feeling that I knew why but it was for a reason so unsavoury that I didn't want to have to think about it until absolutely necessary, or to discuss it with Maeve until I was certain.

Maeve's first few days at St Jacobs unfolded largely as anticipated. It was a continuation of her experiences at the last school, just amplified by the sheer number of pupils. Shockingly, she even encountered a prejudiced teacher who made a disparaging comment about her nationality when she stumbled on a question in class. Despite these challenges, she successfully navigated each day, meeting me in the afternoon after she had finished her paper round. Then, the following Monday, it was my turn to dive into the fray.

On the first morning, I travelled in on bus number 442, a red double-decker which was to be my default mode of transport for the next few years. The school had long days, beginning with the ritual of a compulsory chapel service at 8.30am sharp every day, and woe betide any boy who missed it.

To ensure I arrived on time, I had to get the bus at half past seven from outside the post office, which meant getting up an hour before that. It was the latest bus I could take without risking being late. They ran every twenty minutes but the traffic on the way into Oxford was appalling. Even with the help of a bus lane, it was a minimum of half an hour to get there, and often closer to three-quarters.

At least leaving that early meant I didn't have to run the gauntlet of the village children, to whom I must have stuck out like a sore thumb. It was bad enough the looks I got from the other adults on the bus, as they puffed away on their cigarettes on the top deck, regarding me with disdain. I didn't like having to go up there but, with the lower deck often full, I had no choice.

The school uniform reeked of a privilege I had not been born into. It comprised a maroon and cream blazer with a matching tie and school cap, making me look like some well-to-do child out of an Enid Blyton story. Unsurprisingly, it was also very expensive.

My mother took me to Shepherd & Woodward in Oxford to get me kitted out, the day after she had got back from New York. This included not just the blazer but all the other things I would need, including a P.E. kit in my house colours, and rugby boots. I was in Peel, one of four houses named after prime ministers who had been to Oxford University.

We were under strict orders to arrive at school before half past eight on that first day and were herded swiftly into the imposing hall known as Big John on arrival. It was time for the first of the interminable chapel services that I would be forced to endure for the next few years.

These ceremonies followed an unchanging format. Kev the Rev would appear in the stone pulpit, draped in his white robes, towering over the assembled boys below, to announce the day's hymn. Hastily we would leaf through the weathered songbooks to find it, hoping that the relevant page wouldn't be missing, or so faded as to be illegible, as the organist started up.

Although there were about three hundred hymns in the book, we only ever sang from a selection of about a dozen of them. Today it was 'Onward, Christian Soldiers' which was sung with great gusto by the masters but less so by some of the boys, particularly the older ones, evidently wearied by years of these repetitive proceedings.

After the hymn it was the lesson, read by a sixth-former, which was frequently taken from one of the Bible's darker passages. This preceded a monologue from Kev in which he would lecture us on the evils of some sin or other and what would happen if we committed it. Although it was never explicitly stated, it was frequently the case that he was alluding to his hatred of homosexuals, and the grisly fate that would await any boy in the room who ever dared tread that path.

After the moralising we had prayers, then another hymn, before finally the only vaguely useful part of the process, which was The Master giving out the daily notices. These were often delivered with such a lack of clarity, and in such archaic language, that it wasn't clear exactly what was being announced or what any of us were supposed to be doing about it.

It was half an hour of my life, six days a week, that I would never get back. Afterwards, we returned to our classrooms for registration. A prefect would then call out our names – surnames only, to which the only acceptable response was "Sir!" to reinforce the power trip these sixth-formers were on. They even had the right to punish us, physically, if we were perceived to have done anything wrong.

I could still remember the names of all the boys in my class after all these years, so many times had I sat through this recital. I spent this first roll call looking around the room at the twenty-three others I had shared five years in this purgatory with.

"Ashford."

"Sir!"

"Barrington-Smythe."

"Sir!"

"Beaumont."

"Sir!"

"Cavendish."

"Sir!"

"Fairfax-Carstairs."

"Sir!"

And so on. You get the picture. You could smell the money just in the names, which could have been plucked straight out of an aristocratic costume drama. My bog-standard Taylor raised a few eyebrows right away. I doubt these kids had met many Taylors in the circles they had been brought up in. I might as well have been called Fred Bloggs.

I knew they were going to give me a hard time but I had an ace up my sleeve this time around. I knew all about these boys and what made them tick. I was also aware of who I could trust and who I couldn't. Sadly, in the case of most of them, it was the latter.

Ashford was the son of a Conservative MP and was always boasting that the school would one day have a house named after his father. As for Barrington-Smythe, his father was a top barrister and he was filthy rich, living in a huge house in the poshest part of north Oxford. He was one of the few boys whose first name I did know and it was the most pretentious name you could imagine – Jonty, though I later found out that was short for Jonathan. He even claimed to have servants. When he found out I was from a farming family he delighted in referring to me as "the peasant" for the duration of my time at the school.

The more I looked around the more I wondered what I was letting myself in for by coming back here. I glanced at the bracelet, which was glowing green, trying to reassure me that I was doing the right thing. It didn't appear to have any hard feelings about my attempt to destroy it with a hacksaw a few weeks ago. It had better be a bit more helpful with the mission it had sent me here for because if not, there could be some dark days ahead.

The isolated, elite, and secretive nature of the school made it an ideal haven for sadists, psychopaths, and I'm sorry to say, paedophiles. They could flourish in an institution like this in a way that would have been far more difficult to hide in the mainstream school system. Here they had unchecked power, and it showed. For starters, the level of casual violence from most of the teaching staff was off the scale, and I'm not just talking about giving a kid a clip around the ear or throwing blackboard rubbers.

One of the most feared was Doctor Runcible, aka Rasputin, the ageing history master who despite approaching retirement age still boasted remarkable strength. I can still recall him slamming a boy's head between two sets of lockers as a punishment for wearing headphones in class. Another time, he became so irritated by the hourly chimes on Casio digital watches going off all the time that he said he would smash the next one he heard. This he duly did using a rolling pin which he kept on his desk, presumably for such occasions. With it, he repeatedly smashed at the watch while it was still attached to the unfortunate boy's wrist.

I'm not sure what Runcible had his doctorate in but I'm pretty sure it was nothing medical, given his preference for harm over healing. But unpleasant as he was, his activities paled in comparison to those of Major Kendrick, the P.E. master.

He lacked the academic credentials of the other staff. Whereas they all had countless degrees, published papers, and journals to their name, Kendrick wasn't part of the university establishment. He hailed from Wales where he had spent several years in the military. He was also a proficient rugby player, having played at club level for many years, as well as representing his country on a handful of occasions in the Five Nations. These qualifications made him an ideal candidate, not only for the school's P.E. requirements but also to run the junior cadet force, a long-standing part of the school's traditions.

I don't know what, if any, safeguarding checks existed when Kendrick was appointed but I am guessing they were somewhere between minimal and none. I do know he would never have got a job working with children today if the stories circulating about him were true. But that was seemingly all they were, just rumours, until I heard first-hand years later just what kind of a monster he had been.

After I left the school, I was regularly invited to return for annual events as a member of the Wild Wolves, the name bestowed upon alumni from past years. The name was a nod to the Wolfminster students being liberated from the confines of the institution and thrust into the wild world beyond. For a considerable period, I rebuffed these invitations, harbouring no inclination to cross paths with my snobbish former classmates. Then, one year, I did.

It was the silver anniversary of the year I had started and on a whim, I went along. It wasn't any major commitment, just Christmas drinks in The Bear, a lovely old-fashioned pub a stone's throw from the school. I reasoned that if it was awful I could duck out after one drink. And I almost did when the first two people I encountered were Jonty Barrington-Smythe and Julian Beaumont. They turned out to be even more abhorrent as grown men than they had been as children, banging on about yachts and private jets.

Thankfully, not everyone at Wolfminster was like these two, and I was relieved that night to bump into Steve Savident, or Savvy as he had been known at school. I had more in common with him than the others as he had been one of the kids who had joined with an assisted place at the same time as me. He was refreshingly down to earth compared to the likes of Jonty and had gone on to work in the drinks industry for one of the national breweries after school. However, on the night of the reunion he seemed nervous, almost jumpy, and after a few drinks I found out why.

He was keen to talk to me, and finding a quiet table in the corner, it all came out. Child sexual abuse wasn't something that was talked about much in my youth, but by the mid-2000s more and more stories were starting to come out about people in positions of trust abusing young people.

Steve had decided he couldn't stay silent any longer. It had been Mr Keats who had persuaded him. Good old Mr Keats – or young Mr Keats as he had been when we had known him. He had started at the school on the same day as us, at the tender age of twenty-two, which made him less than half the age of most of the staff. He had replaced Mr Carmichael, a deceased contemporary of literary lights such as T.S. Eliot and C.S. Lewis who had taught at Wolfminster from 1926 to 1981. It truly was a job for life once you were part of the furniture. No one ever retired from Wolfminster if they didn't want to.

Keats was an exception, sacked in 2002, an unprecedented occurrence. Savvy explained to me that our former English master had become aware of the sordid activities of Kendrick and had tried to expose him. He hadn't had much joy and soon found himself the subject of a witch hunt and thrown out of the school amid accusations of corruption and embezzlement. No criminal charges were ever brought but the situation was clear. Those who ran Wolfminster had closed ranks to protect the school's reputation, leaving further generations of children at risk.

Keats had since been trying to build a case against Kendrick by approaching ex-students like Savvy to try to uncover past abuse. It turned out there were dozens of victims but before it could go any further, Kendrick died of a heart attack on the rugby field at the age of sixty-eight, and that was the end of that. Until now.

What if I could do something about it? The bracelet certainly seemed to think I could because it pulsed green at the thought, but it was going to be a tall order. If Keats, a grown man employed by the school, hadn't been able to do anything about it even after twenty years working alongside Kendrick, what hope did I have?

I would figure something out. I had done it before, against the odds, and I could do it again. In the meantime, I had my hands full just dealing with the day-to-day realities of surviving at the school. I had anticipated a smoother ride this time around. However, after my first run-in with Jonty and his upper-crust chums on that first day, I realised it might not be as plain sailing as I had thought.

It was the lunch break and I was chatting in our classroom with Savvy, who I decided to befriend as soon as I could, seeing him as a potential ally. Then Jonty and Julian walked in, saw us, and came over. We hadn't spoken to each other properly before this point, having spent all morning in lessons, but judging by their swagger as they came over, they had already figured out they were way above us on the social scale. Now they had decided it was time to put us in our place, because that's how people like them operated.

"I say, you there. Taylor, isn't it? Tell me, what does your daddy do?"

I wasn't going to try to be clever so I decided to just answer honestly and see what snooty claptrap came back in return. "He's a carpenter," I replied.

"A carpenter? That's manual work, isn't it? Do you hear this, Julian? Fancy that, here at Wolfminster. Blue collar chaps."

"Don't knock it, Jonty," said Julian. "I mean someone's got to fix the lavatories, haven't they?"

"That would be a plumber, not a carpenter," I replied.

"Whatever," said Jonty. "It's all manual working-class stuff, isn't it? Well, I'm sorry to have to inform you that you won't be getting any woodwork classes or learning how to mend toilets at this school. The sort of people who come here do not need to acquire such skills. We pay poor people to do those things for us."

"Good job we've got Latin to fill the gap, eh?" I replied jovially. "I am sure that will come in very useful in the future."

I laced my words with sarcasm but he didn't seem to pick up on it.

"Quite right," said Jonty. "And what about your mother? Let me guess, she works in a shop, right? One of those frightful supermarket places like that one in Westgate where they wear those horrible brown and orange uniforms."

"Actually, she's a painter," I replied.

"A painter, indeed. You know, that could come in handy. Mummy was only saying the other day that the scullery needed a lick of paint. How much does she charge an hour?"

I had chosen the wrong word and needed to clarify. "When I said painter, I meant artist. She paints pictures and is quite famous as it happens. She's just had an exhibition in New York."

"Oh, really?" asked Jonty, briefly dropping the condescending sneer as he considered the possibility I might not just be some country bumpkin after all. "What's her name? Maybe I'll have heard of her."

"Mary Cartwright," I replied, using the name she had chosen to be known by in the art world.

"Cartwright?" he questioned, eyes lighting up as he sensed an opportunity. "But your name is Taylor. Are you illegitimate or something?"

"No," I attempted to explain. "What it is…"

And that was as far as I got, because at that point Jonty jumped up onto a chair and shouted out to the dozen or so kids in the room, "Listen to this, everybody! Taylor here is a bastard!"

And they all cheered and started laughing at me, even Savvy, who I had hoped might be the one person to stick up for me.

It had been an inauspicious start.

October 1981

Over the years, I had often reflected on my time at Wolfminster and wondered if I had been overly critical. Was it truly as dreadful as my memories suggested?

No, it wasn't. It was worse!

Apart from its prestigious alumni and reputation, the school lacked any redeeming qualities. Nearly everyone within its walls was unlikeable, from the pampered, pretentious pupils to the condescending masters. In between dishing out violent punishments, they flaunted their intellectual superiority at every opportunity, liking nothing better than to put those beneath them in their place.

There were a handful of exceptions. The most recent recruitment to the teaching ranks, Mr Keats, stood out among his colleagues as a decent individual. He shunned violence and took a genuine interest in the welfare of the pupils in his care. It was a wonder he even secured the position, considering the old-school-tie mentality that permeated the institution. This might have been because the school needed to find someone at very short notice, with old Carmichael keeling over barely a week before term was due to start.

The appointment of a young, fresh-faced teacher might have seemed as though it was ushering in the winds of change but it was a false dawn. After his arrival, the teaching staff remained unchanged during my five years there, all male of course. Female teaching staff were unheard of. It was rather like one of those crusty old golf clubs that refuse to allow women members.

As for the boys, not all of them were as reprehensible as Jonty and Julian. The few decent types amongst my peers tended to keep their heads down and get on with things. They knew better than to attract the attention of those two, who had quickly established themselves at the top of the food chain. That was the way it was at Wolfminster. There was a pecking order and you were expected to know where you were in it and stay in your lane. Which in my case meant crawling along on the hard shoulder.

Despite my facing their derision on the first day, Jonty and Julian largely left me alone in the weeks that followed. I was helped by the bracelet which assisted me in avoiding them and alerting me to potential issues. They tended to wander the corridors and classrooms at lunchtime looking for people to torment. If they didn't encounter me, then some other kids would get picked on instead.

When I wasn't dodging them, I was evading trouble closer to home. One night, I had a dream that I would run into Martin and some new friends of his when I got off the bus after school. They were delighted to encounter the posh kid who was different to them and relished every moment when they were beating me up, ripping my blazer and pushing me into the pond on the village green.

I knew this dream was no idle warning because this incident had already occurred, all those years ago. This time, I was able to avoid it. There were four bus stops in the village so I just got off at an earlier one, further from home, and walked back a different way.

I might have escaped a beating but none of this was doing much for my self-esteem. Running and hiding all the time was no way to live, and I continued to rue my decision to go to Wolfminster. But there was no point moaning about it now. What was done was done, and I was hardly likely to be given a third chance to come back and do it all over again.

At least the bracelet was more helpful at school than it had been during the events of the summer. It had assisted in the entrance exam back in March and was doing the same now in lessons, providing answers and guidance, and I certainly needed it. Other than mathematics, where my natural ability shone through, I found the curriculum challenging, particularly Latin, a subject I had struggled with the first time I came to Wolfminster.

I started at a natural disadvantage thanks to my late introduction to the language, unlike many of my well-heeled classmates who had been studying it since their prep school days. I just could not get to grips with all those weird tenses and archaic texts.

It didn't help that the whole process of studying the subject in the first place seemed utterly ludicrous to me. What was the point of learning a language that died out centuries ago? When Jonty overheard me making this point to Savvy in the lunch hall one day, he said I didn't understand because of my lack of cultural refinement. I didn't bother arguing.

It was the only O-Level that I failed, and the five years of study I had done forty years ago were of no help now whatsoever. I had forgotten the lot, which just goes to show how much use I had made of Latin in my adult life. If it were not for the bracelet's help I would have been truly hopeless, which would have invited the wrath of Remus, the nickname of our sadistic Latin master.

Mr Remington, as he was otherwise known, was ranked by the boys as the third most violent teacher in the school after Runcible and Kendrick. His preferred method of punishment was a ruler across the knuckles which could be administered for as little as getting the conjugation of a verb wrong.

Thankfully, the bracelet came to my aid so when I was asked to conjugate the verb 'to walk'. I was able to confidently say "*ambulo, ambulas, ambulat*," and so on, without a hint of hesitation. Without it, I would have gone home with sore fingers every day.

Because of my decent performance in class, Jonty and the other snobs eased off on me a bit, and with me also able to avoid them during breaks, I was able to turn my attention to the unpleasant task of dealing with Major Kendrick.

Quite how I was to undertake the daunting task of putting a stop to him, I hadn't yet figured out. But it had to be done. That was why I had come back to Wolfminster, after all. Even without the sexual abuse, the man was a violent bully, as he amply demonstrated during those first few weeks.

We had P.E. twice a week, which in the Michaelmas term was heavily focused on rugby. This was no surprise, given Kendrick's background. Saturday morning lessons would always be outside, taking the form of a rugby match using the university's pitches. Kendrick usually participated in these matches which was bad news for any pupil who wasn't on his team.

In midweek, we alternated between using a college gym for indoor training and outdoor rugby practice. Whatever we were doing, participation was compulsory, regardless of the weather conditions and our state of health, as one of my classmates discovered to his detriment on the first Wednesday in October.

We had assembled in the gym for some circuit training, and as soon as Kendrick came in wearing his trademark red Adidas tracksuit, his eyes alighted on the one boy still in his school uniform. Immediately, he berated the outlier in his Welsh accent.

"Pankhurst! Why aren't you in your P.E. kit, boy?"

"Please, sir, I've got a really bad cold," replied Pankhurst, adding a couple of well-timed coughs to add credence to his claim. "I've got a note from my mum asking if I can be excused."

"A cold?" enquired Kendrick. "A cold?" When Kendrick was angry, he tended to repeat himself, with subsequent iterations increasingly louder than the first to emphasise his mounting displeasure.

Meanwhile, the class emitted a few titters of laughter, joining forces against the boy who had been singled out by Kendrick as today's runt of the litter. This was largely down to relief that it was someone else in his sights rather than them.

"Yes, here it is, sir," said Pankhurst, nervously handing over the note to Kendrick, who snatched it out of his hand and began reading it out loud, deliberately adopting a high-pitched and feeble-sounding tone as he spoke.

"Dear Mister Kendrick. Rupert is feeling poorly today so please can he be excused from gym. Yours sincerely, Mrs Pankhurst."

As he finished reading the note, he screwed it up into a ball and threw it away into the corner of the gym.

"Come here, boy," he bellowed at Pankhurst, who had been slowly backing away since handing Kendrick the note. The terrified child almost tiptoed towards him, wide-eyed with fear. All the boys in the class had heard about Kendrick's fearsome reputation from the older pupils, and this was the first time they were to witness him in his full fury.

"Yes, go on, Ru-pert," mocked Jonty, elongating the first syllable with exaggerated tenderness, mimicking the tone of a mother coaxing a reluctant child.

This drew more laughs from the other boys. Jonty knew he was on safe ground because he had been buttering Kendrick up ever since he had arrived at the school, showing an interest in, and flattering him about his rugby career. Even at this age, Jonty was already well-versed in the skills of social climbing.

When Pankhurst reached Kendrick, the master towered over him and lifted him effortlessly into the air by his tie, leaving the hapless boy choking and gagging for air. It wasn't difficult to imagine Kendrick playing for Wales back in the day – he was built like the proverbial brick shithouse and the skinny Pankhurst looked like a tiny, wriggling mouse being picked up by his tail in comparison.

"Firstly, you can tell your mother my title is Major, not Mister. I didn't spend nine years in the army to be referred to by a title fit only for lily-livered civvies. And if you are well enough to come to school, you are well enough for P.E. Is that clear?"

Pankhurst merely emitted a gargled gasp, his face turning purple as he gasped for air.

"I'll take that as a yes," he added, letting go, leaving the boy to drop to the floor where he collapsed in a heap, almost losing consciousness after his ordeal.

"Pathetic creature," said Kendrick, revelling in the child's suffering. "I don't know what we're breeding these days. It's high time this country brought back National Service. Now get that uniform off and join in with the rest of us. You can do P.E. in your pants today."

None of the class showed the slightest sympathy for Pankhurst's predicament. Most of them took pleasure in it, continuing to torment him with jibes after we went out to the rugby pitch. Exposed to the elements, he looked like death warmed up as he shivered in the chilly October breeze dressed in just a white vest, and a sky-blue pair of Marks & Spencer's Y-fronts.

Unlike most of the teachers at the school, who rated the boys on a combination of their academic ability and what their parents did for a living, Kendrick judged them purely on their physical attributes and sporting ability. Jonty and Julian had nothing to worry about as they were keen and competent rugby players. But those he identified as weaklings, or who showed a penchant for the wrong sport, would all incur his wrath sooner or later.

The next unfortunate to come into his crosshairs was McKenzie, the son of a Scottish laird. Hailing from the Highlands, he was one of a handful of kids in my class who had the misfortune to be boarders. It was bad enough having to come to the school in the daytime so I couldn't even begin to envisage how awful their life must be, cramped into the tiny dormitories that served as their living quarters. At least I got to go home in the evenings.

He brought his run-in with Kendrick upon himself. It happened the week after the Pankhurst incident, when he dared to ask a question that sent the Major almost paralytic with rage.

Kendrick had been banging on about line-out techniques in the gym before we headed outside to practice, at which point he asked the class if they had any questions. Few ever did unless they were of the arse-kissing variety from Jonty or Julian. However, McKenzie unwisely put his hand up, and when permitted to speak came out with something that was like pouring petrol on a barbecue.

"Sir, I was just wondering. Rugby is great but is there any chance we could play football one week?"

The reaction on Kendrick's face was immediate. It was one of shock and disbelief that anyone would even dare ask such a thing.

"I beg your pardon," said Kendrick, fixing the boy's eyes with an intense gaze that did not bode well. "Did I hear you correctly, boy? Did you just ask if you could play with a round ball?"

"Well, I…" began McKenzie before Kendrick interrupted him.

"A round ball? A r-r-r-round ball!" Kendrick's eyes were almost popping out of his head in anger.

The boys watched, fascinated. When Kendrick rolled his R's and exaggerated his Welsh accent to this extent, trouble was sure to follow. Realising his mistake, McKenzie tried to backtrack but it was too late.

"Sorry, it was just an idea, don't worry about it, sir," he said, backing away, the memory of what had happened to Pankhurst just seven days earlier no doubt in his mind. But it was far, far too late.

"I'll give you a round ball, boy!" yelled Kendrick, plucking a medicine ball from a shelf at the side of the gym and hurling it at McKenzie with ease, striking him full in the stomach. He went down as if he had been shot, and promptly vomited all over the floor.

"Soccer is for pansies," declared Kendrick, standing over McKenzie who was doubled over in agony as he writhed at his feet. "Never let me hear it mentioned again. Now get a mop and bucket and clean that mess up."

And so it went on, week after week, one abusive incident after another. Someone always fell foul of him though with the help of the bracelet I managed to avoid it being me. But his bullying in the gym was only the tip of the iceberg.

The most disturbing thing he did occurred every Saturday after rugby when we would be inevitably caked in mud. Then we were forced to run the gauntlet of taking a shower, naked, under Kendrick's supervision. These facilities were set in a U-shaped corridor which we entered at one end and exited at the other. There were six showers spaced out at regular intervals which were in serious need of maintenance. The water was tepid at best and came out pathetically slowly, often little more than a trickle.

We were told to line up and sent through at ten-second intervals, timed by Kendrick on his stopwatch, giving us around a minute each under the feeble flow. It was just about enough to get the worst of the mud off and that was all. But it was the behaviour of Kendrick that was of most concern. As we entered, he stood by the entrance and made inappropriate and creepy remarks about the state of each boy's development, such as noting who had started growing pubic hair and who hadn't.

Remarkably, no one ever said anything about this or even seemed to realise how wrong it was. None of us had received any sex education by this age, so unlike in the twenty-first century, where children are clued up at a much younger age, we didn't recognise the warning signs.

I barely even knew what child abuse was when I was that age the first time around. The only clues I had gleaned were from public information films on television featuring a boy and his cat, Charley, urging kids not to take sweets from strange men.

Now, the second time around, I felt as sick as McKenzie had been on the gym floor as I observed Kendrick looking where he shouldn't. Even given my previous innocence, how could I not have noticed this? It was disgusting and merely heightened my resolve to put a stop to him.

While I was trying to figure out how, there was no shortage of things to do closer to home, starting the day after the medicine ball incident. That night I had another dream in which Maeve had been out doing her evening paper round when she was confronted by Carey and her gang. They knocked her off her bicycle, beat her up, and then threw her newspapers and bike into the Thames, never to be seen again.

When I awoke, I was certain it would happen that day. I even knew exactly where and when but there was a problem. Maeve would be cycling down the towpath towards the lock house when she would encounter her tormentors. If I was there I could prevent it but there was an issue in terms of time. It was all going to happen about 4 o'clock, and the earliest bus I could catch back from Oxford didn't get in until half past.

Alternatively, I could warn her to steer clear of the towpath before I went to school but there was no answer when I called her house. I guessed she was out on her morning paper round and her mother must have left for work already.

I contemplated going out to try to find her, or perhaps putting a note through her door, but there simply wasn't enough time. I would miss my bus and be late which would probably mean an after-school detention. That wouldn't help Maeve. I decided instead to head off to school on time, and then try to sneak out early.

Not for the first time, I despaired at how difficult it was to communicate in the 1980s. This sort of thing wouldn't be a problem in the future with mobile phones, SMS, Facebook, and a myriad other ways to instantly contact people. But today, the only way I would be able to warn her was by being there in person at 4 o'clock.

How was I going to get out of school? Quite easily. Just like my primary school, anyone could walk in or out at their leisure, which is exactly what I did during the afternoon break. It meant I would be absent from double Latin which would surely lead to punishment the next day but I'd worry about that later. The important thing was that I was on the half past two bus home, which was a surprise to my mother when I walked into the kitchen at about ten past three.

"Why are you home so early?" she asked. "It's not a half-day is it?"

"No," I replied. "I'm answering the call of the bracelet. Maeve's in trouble and I've got to go and help her. I bunked off the last lesson."

Bunking off was the popular expression for skipping school when I was a kid. I don't know where it came from but they said it a lot on *Grange Hill*.

"I see," she said. "Best you go and do what you need to do, then. What did you tell the school?"

"Nothing. I just slipped out when they weren't looking."

"Won't you be in trouble tomorrow?"

"Probably."

"Well, don't worry about that. I'll sort it out. You go and help Maeve." Good old Mum. Since I'd saved her life she had been right by my side. I hadn't told her about Kendrick, though. There was too much chance she would insist on reporting him herself, or even pulling me out of the school for my own protection, which might mess up whatever the bracelet had in mind.

I whizzed upstairs to get changed, intending to intercept Maeve at the school gates. There was no way I was going up to St Jacobs in my Wolfminster uniform. Never mind rescuing Maeve, I'd be the one getting lynched the second they saw my blazer.

As I approached the school gates, I realised I had left it too late. A flood of pupils was already cascading outwards like a burst dam, their lively chatter filling the air. I couldn't see Maeve anywhere among the bustling throng but a couple of kids I recognised from my old school spotted me, and even without my uniform, one of them immediately shouted out, "Hey look, there's that posh kid."

I slunk backwards, looking for a little cover behind some parked cars on the other side of the road. It was bad enough that these two had seen me but if I ran into Martin there would be real trouble. He had been spoiling for an opportunity to have a go at me for weeks. I had managed to avoid him until now but Simon had taken great pleasure in telling me that Martin was going to 'do me over' the next time he saw me.

I saw Martin and Philip come out but they didn't see me from my vantage point behind a rusting Cortina. Shortly afterwards, out came Carey and her entourage, wandering down the road in the opposite direction to Martin.

As they walked, I saw Jane handing around sticks of Wrigley's which they popped into their mouths, promptly chucking the wrappers on the ground. So much for keeping Britain tidy. I cast aside any lingering thoughts of trying to find Maeve and instead began to follow Carey's group at a discreet distance.

Even from fifty yards or more behind, I could hear the racket they were making, laughing, shouting, and swearing. They had juvenile delinquency written all over them, amply demonstrated by one of the girls I hadn't seen before who decided to pull a wing mirror off a yellow Citroen 2CV, to much appreciation from the others.

Carey was at the front of the group, walking confidently as befitted her status as their leader. I crept closer as she led them away from the populated part of the village along the public footpath that led to the river. As soon as they were out of sight of the street, she produced a pack of John Player Specials, the distinctive black and gold packaging recognisable even from afar as the livery of the Lotus Formula One car driven by Nigel Mansell.

She handed them around to her three accomplices, who spat out their gum before lighting up like seasoned smokers. How long had this been going on? Not yet twelve years old, some of them, and already they had been seduced by the allure of cigarettes.

I did not need to follow them any further as the footpath only went to the river, and I already knew that was where they were headed. It would be quicker for me if I cut back towards the road bridge where I could head Maeve off before she turned onto the towpath. I timed this to perfection because just as I reached the bridge, she pedalled into view, on her way to deliver the *Oxford Mail* to Les, our local lockkeeper.

"Maeve!" I called out, stopping in her tracks as she brought the bicycle to a shuddering halt in front of me. She was in jeans and a green jumper, a more practical outfit for delivering papers than her usual dresses, with the branded orange bag of the local rag draped over her shoulder.

Just like my mother earlier, she expressed surprise at seeing me. I quickly explained but was surprised by her reaction.

"I don't know, Nick, perhaps I should just face them. I mean, it's all very well you doing your knight in shining armour bit but what's going to happen come January when you go back to the future? I'll need to learn to stand on my own two feet."

"The bracelet disagrees," I said, noting it glowing red at her words. "Yes, I see what you're saying about dealing with them in the long term but today's not the day to have that confrontation. You're outnumbered and isolated away from the village. If you go down there it's going to end badly."

"And what about tomorrow? And the next day?"

"Chances are, they might not come down here again. Have you seen them here before?"

"No, never," she replied. "But what about Les's paper? He'll be on the phone complaining to the shop if he doesn't get it. He went mad on my first week when he got the *Sunday Mirror* instead of the *News of the World*. That was the fault of the shop, not me, I hasten to add."

"I'll take it to him," I said. "Just for today. I don't think they'll come back again."

"And if they do?"

"We'll cross that bridge when we come to it."

"Now you're the one doing an Edith!" she exclaimed, laughing at my use of the cliché.

211

"Bloody hell, I am, aren't I?" I replied as she reached into the bag and handed me a copy of the paper. Doing an Edith was an in-joke we had come up with whenever one of us came out with a proverb or an old wives' tale.

"I'll go and finish the rest of my round, and we'll meet back at yours later," said Maeve. "But be careful. I don't want you facing off with them and being the one ending up in the river."

"I'm not afraid of them," I replied, and I wasn't. However, as I approached the lock I couldn't deny that their aggressive demeanour was a little intimidating. As I got closer, I could hear their cackles, even against the strong whooshing sound of the nearby weir as the river rushed through it.

"Well, look who's here," called out Jane, as I strode up the towpath, carrying Les's paper. "It's Little Lord Fauntleroy."

"Where's your girlfriend?" shouted Carey, taking a long draw on her cigarette whilst fiddling about with the latch that kept one of the black and white lock gates secured.

Did they know that Maeve came down here to deliver papers? Was that why she had asked? My gut feeling suggested that wasn't the case and they had only asked because of my association with her. I didn't need to come up with an answer because, at that moment, Les emerged from the keeper's house.

"Is that my paper?" he asked, as I walked towards him. "You're late. Where's the usual girl?"

"She's indisposed," I said, just as Les clocked Carey and her mates messing around with the gates.

"Oi! What the bloody hell do you think you're doing?" he yelled. Les was a big man with a powerful set of lungs and he certainly got their attention.

"What's it to you, old man?" yelled Carey, looking for appreciation from her gang of thugs. But what Les said next quickly put a stop to her bravado.

"Well, well. Carey Evans. Our carnival queen. Look at you that day, all dressed up like butter wouldn't melt, representing the village, and look at the state of you now. Does your father know you smoke?"

She cast her eyes down to the ground and said nothing.

"I'm guessing he doesn't but he soon will. Did you know we were on the same darts team at The Farmers Arms? No, I didn't think you did. Now scram, the lot of you, and don't ever let me see you messing around down here again."

He snatched the paper from my hands without so much as a thank you and stomped back inside, as the girls ran off up the towpath. That had gone better than anticipated and the bracelet was glowing green at the outcome.

Carey had been taken down a peg or two, and what's more, now she knew of Les's connection to her father, she was unlikely to come down here again. Maeve would have nothing more to worry about, not while delivering Les his paper, anyway.

But something she had said before was preying on my mind. She was right, I was going back soon and with no bracelet to fall back on, both she and I would have to learn to stand on our own two feet.

November 1981

Mum wrote a convincing letter for me to take to school explaining that I'd needed to leave early for a dentist appointment, but it didn't do me any good. I still got rapped across the knuckles by Remus with his ruler. He took great delight in informing me that any absence had to be authorised in advance, not afterwards.

Mercifully, it was then half-term. For me, this fell in the first week of November. Wolfminster seemed to delight in deliberately structuring term dates so that they did not align with those of the other schools in the area. It was no concern of theirs if it caused a logistical headache for parents who had kids at different schools.

It meant that Maeve and I were unable to spend as much time together during those two weeks as we would have liked. She was off the first week and me the second but we still got together some evenings. On the last day of October, we had been out trick-or-treating, though the pickings on Meadowbrook Lane were mostly lean, despite Maeve putting a decent effort into her costume.

Halloween back in 1981 was nothing like the crazy marketing event it would later become. There was zero merchandise in the shops, and any children wanting to dress up had to make their own costumes. As for trick-or-treating, I'm not sure if this was widespread across the country at the time but I know we started doing it in our village sometime in the late 1970s. It caught on to the extent that by my last year of primary school, Mr Jones was denouncing the practice in assembly.

Since she had been labelled a Banshee so often by the girls at school, Maeve had decided she might as well dress up as one. She had a real aptitude for creating costumes, and with her mother's assistance had made a stunning outfit. Thus, she turned up in a flowing, tattered gown in shades of midnight blue and deep purple, with a veil made of black cotton to give her a mystical air. My effort was lame by comparison; just an old white sheet with two eye holes poked in it.

Edith's contribution when we knocked on her door was predictably paltry. She gave us two New Berry Fruits, which I considered to be revolting concoctions even when fresh out of the box. They were even worse when dried up and almost inedible, as these two were. I strongly suspected that they were left over from the previous Christmas. Then she gave us a lecture, saying she didn't approve of Halloween because it was ungodly. Simon wasn't allowed to participate, we were lucky to be getting anything at all, and she wouldn't be opening the door to anyone else.

Edith deserved a trick played on her for being so miserable but I resisted the temptation, recalling the trouble I had got into the previous year when Martin had decided it would be a great idea to egg all the houses we visited that didn't answer the door. That included Honeysuckle, which caused some right ructions when Stan came after us. Fortunately, I got away with it because I was in costume and he didn't know it was me.

We wisely avoided his place this time, and also swerved Sunflower, though we saw Brenda nosing through the window as we passed. Didn't that woman ever sit down?

William and Jackie were the most generous on the lane, giving us both an Aero and a packet of Opal Fruits. Visiting the houses on the street where Maeve lived proved to be more fruitful so we were able to gorge ourselves silly on sugar back at her house afterwards. It seemed my sweet tooth had returned, having lost it as an adult. When it came to physical things such as taste buds, my eleven-year-old body usually held the ascendancy over my middle-aged brain.

When it came to more cerebral matters, the reverse was usually true, with going trick-or-treating being a good example. Despite the ten months I had spent back in my childhood body, fitting in by playing football with my mates and other things that kids do, I was still very much aware that I was at heart a man in his fifties. Every day, I still felt twinges of imposter syndrome. I might be acting like a kid, stuffing my face with sweets but in truth I was still an adult trapped in a child's body.

On the way back from Maeve's that night I passed the pub which heightened those feelings as the laughter and chatter of people having fun carried outside. It brought it all home, that here I was, pretending to be a kid in my crappy Halloween costume, while there was a grown man inside me yearning to go in for a pint.

After the weekend, Maeve went back to school, and I was left to my own devices for a week, though I did spend some of that time lending a hand on the farm. Then, midweek, Mum told me something that I didn't want to hear.

"Your father wants to see you," she said, over breakfast after I had come back from helping William milk the cows.

"Well, I don't want to see him," I retorted and with good reason. I had only seen him a couple of times since his departure, in the form of incredibly stilted and uncomfortable afternoons in the park during the summer holidays. It didn't feel to me like he was that interested in seeing me on either of those occasions.

"I think you should," she said. "As you know, I've instigated divorce proceedings and we're going to have to talk about custody and visitation rights."

"There's no question of who gets custody. I'm staying here with you."

As I spoke, a sense of trepidation came over me at the thought of the hideous alternative. I had already endured life being brought up by Dad and Tracy once and it was an experience I had no desire to repeat.

"Yes, that's already been decided," she said, much to my relief. "But he still has a right to see you."

"Does he even want to?" I asked, remembering how besotted he had been with Tracy to my detriment during my teenage years. "Or is he just doing it out of a sense of guilt or duty?"

"Both, probably. But look, he is still your father whatever he might have done. It can't hurt to see him, can it?"

"I suppose not," I said, without a hint of enthusiasm. Therefore, on Thursday evening, I was sent over to the flat they were renting in a rough part of the village to have a meal with them.

They were living on the top floor of a three-storey featureless concrete block and a dismal place it was too. Three or four dogs were barking incessantly as I arrived, the falling darkness adding to the sense of gloom the whole area was giving off.

As I entered the hallway, my nostrils were assailed by the unwelcome combination of tobacco smoke and stale cooking which I soon realised permeated the entire building. Halfway up the filthy stairwell was a puddle, and I am pretty sure it wasn't water. These flats were only about fifteen years old but already showed signs of decay everywhere, from flaky paint to patches of black mould on the walls.

My visit was a forced and painful experience from the outset. Tracy made it abundantly clear that she didn't want me there, and had made no effort to cook a meal. Instead, we ate from the recently opened Chinese takeaway nearby. The food, though decent, did little to thaw the icy atmosphere in the tiny flat. I did my best to try to make conversation but it was impossible to get anything flowing.

"So, how's work?" I probed, attempting to break the uncomfortable silence that hung in the air.

"Slow," replied Dad, his tone subdued. I couldn't help but consider how much of his current employment woes were down to the scandal that had tarnished his reputation in the village. He had always had plenty of work before, certainly enough for him and Tracy to afford to live somewhere better than this dump.

I had to question how much longer their relationship was going to last, having already seen overwhelming evidence that Tracy was a gold-digger on the day of his death at the hospital. And that was in the old world where he still owned Wisteria and had a thriving profession. She had stayed with that version of him until the end but how differently would she perceive him now in these reduced circumstances?

Tracy stopped short of showing any outright hostility in front of my father but the message was clear on her face throughout the evening, which had 'fuck off' written all over it. It was as clear as if it had been tattooed on her forehead. After about half an hour of excruciating conversation that bordered on the monosyllabic, I couldn't wait to get out of there. I made a lazy excuse about having some homework to do, even though it was half-term but they probably didn't know that. Before I left, Tracy made her position on my visit clear.

"Don't come back here again, you little tosser," she said when my father popped to the loo and we were briefly left alone together.

"I've no intention of doing so," I replied. "Why would I want to hang out in a shithole like this with a slag like you?"

She got up, and I thought she was going to hit me again, just like the night she had first babysat, but at that moment my father came back into the room. It annoyed me that he seemed completely oblivious to what was going on, and that was more than enough for me. I put my shoes and coat on, took my leave and hot-footed it down the stairs, taking care not to step in the puddle which appeared to have grown since my arrival.

I couldn't wait to get outside into the fresh night air, away from the stinky building and the poisonous atmosphere in the flat. I wanted to get home as quickly as my legs could carry me so took a shortcut across the park, skirting around a group of older teenagers who were busy swigging from cans of Skol and setting off fireworks. As soon I was past them, I tucked my parka tightly around me and ran, not stopping until I made it safely back to the comfort of the roaring fire. We lit this every night now as the weather grew colder.

After the weekend, it was back to school and time to face up to the task I knew was coming. I feared it was going to be an arduous and dangerous process but thankfully, this time the bracelet guided me through the plan in fine detail. It didn't just drop ambiguous hints here and there but told me exactly what to do and when to do it.

Kendrick spent a lot of time in the cadet office, a space he had effectively made his own. He had even ostentatiously had his nameplate put on the door. Behind the office, via a connecting door, was a darkroom which had been created by the art department some years ago. It was seldom used.

It was here that he carried out his vile acts. I knew this because the bracelet had played out various scenarios to me in dreams. Thankfully, it had spared me any graphic details about exactly what went on behind the closed door of the darkroom but it wasn't difficult to connect the dots.

The school had numerous societies that pupils could join, many of which Kendrick was the patron of. These covered topics from astronomy to zoology, and many were dormant, having been formed years ago by long-gone Wild Wolves. So, if a pupil did develop an interest in a niche hobby, such as stamp collecting, chances are he would find his way to Kendrick's door.

Through a combination of cunning and intimidation, he had never been caught. Either his victims were too terrified to make a complaint, or the claims were dismissed due to lack of evidence. And so, the abuse continued. Even Mr Keats hadn't been able to stop him, even though he had figured out exactly what was going on. But Mr Keats hadn't had the benefit of the bracelet.

The device on my wrist had given me the time, location, and the plan I needed to acquire the evidence. All I needed to do was enter the office at a specific time, conceal my cassette player in the darkroom, and set it to record. Provided I followed the instructions to the letter, I would not be caught. I entered the office at precisely 12.43pm on Thursday and was out again within three minutes. Nobody saw me enter or leave. Then, I retrieved my recorder at the end of the day.

The contents of the tape were damning and worse than anything I could have expected. I only listened to it once and never wanted to hear it again. However, I couldn't hand it over to anyone just yet. I had to make backup copies first which I did using Maeve's twin-deck cassette player. I had used a C-90 tape for the initial recording but there were only a few minutes that needed copying. It was all there, the coercion, the intimidation, and the crime itself, followed by the threats of what would happen if the boy ever told. It was more than enough for a judge to throw away the key.

I made two copies, both onto cheap C-15 cassettes that were aimed at the software market. Both were dubbed with the volume on zero. It would still record; we just would not hear it. Maeve was with me, and there was no way I was going to expose her to any of it, even though she was fully aware of what I was doing and why.

The bracelet was specific about what I needed to do with my copies of the tape. One needed to be passed to Mr Keats, but not personally. I had to leave it in his pigeonhole at school, sealed in an envelope, at a precise time to ensure he received it. He was not to know it had come from me. The other was to be posted to a senior police officer in Oxford, whose name was given to me by the bracelet. From that point onwards, my involvement was at an end.

All I could do now was wait and see what happened next. The bracelet was offering no further information. A few days went by but no police cars came down Merton Street, sirens blazing, to drag him off in cuffs. It was something of an anti-climax, and by the end of the following week, nothing had changed. Then, suddenly, after the weekend, Kendrick wasn't there anymore. There was a new P.E. master, a younger and far more amenable chap who reminded me of good old Mr West from my primary school days.

Kendrick's swift disappearance and sudden replacement were never mentioned by the school. Nothing was said during the morning notices in Big John about him, nor was the appointment of his successor even announced. It was as if the new man had been there all along. Strangely, it was barely even discussed among the boys.

I noticed on that first day that all trace of his existence had disappeared from the school, from the timetables displayed on the main noticeboard to the removal of his name from the cadet office door. I was consumed with curiosity about exactly what had happened and toyed with the idea of asking Mr Keats about it. However, the bracelet glowed red to make it clear that on no account was I to do that. And in this pre-internet era, I couldn't just go online to try to find out what had become of him.

All I could do was scour the local and national press for any mention of a teacher being investigated or arrested but there was nothing. It was as if he had vanished off the face of the earth, and after a few weeks, I began to wonder if that had indeed been his fate.

I knew from my time at Wolfminster what a secretive institution it was and how much it protected its reputation. I believe that's why Mr Keats had run into brick walls on the previous occasion when he had tried to bring Kendrick to justice, costing him his job in the process. It had been less damaging for the school to get rid of Keats than Kendrick.

It made me question how much those in charge knew about Kendrick's activities, and what else they might be covering up. I hadn't been led to investigate any other dark deeds within the walls of the school but I suspected that there were plenty of other skeletons in the closet. In this case, the evidence on the tape was so damning that certain people in positions of power had decided that Kendrick had to go – permanently. That way, they could avoid any scandal or anyone coming sniffing around who might get a whiff of those other skeletons.

The lack of police presence or press coverage, and how quickly all traces of him had been erased from the school, had inevitably led me to this conclusion. Kendrick hadn't just disappeared, he had been disappeared, in a wearing-concrete-boots, sleeping-with-the-fishes, kind of way. Which, quite frankly, was fine by me. He was a horrible man who deserved everything he had got.

Whatever his fate, I was just glad that it had all gone so smoothly in comparison to earlier tasks. It was a great relief to know that Savvy, and numerous others in the future, would no longer suffer at his hands. I knew there were others like Kendrick out there committing similar crimes, and I couldn't stop them all but at least I had stopped one of them.

As for all those other skeletons, it looked like they would be staying buried for now. I had no doubt there were all sorts of other dodgy things going on at Wolfminster that I could have investigated but I was running out of time. Where did all the money from the astronomical fees go? Someone was creaming it off somewhere, while we ate food not much better than gruel, and sat on nineteenth-century furniture riddled with woodworm.

Whoever it was, it was a fair bet it was the same person or people who had authorised Kendrick's demise. I still had many unanswered questions about that. Who was the police superintendent I had been told to send the tape to, and what was his link to the school? Why also give it to Keats, newly appointed, and hardly in an influential position? Was it because he was the only one who wouldn't try to sweep it under the carpet? My imagination ran into overdrive for a while, inventing a secret cabal of shadowy figures in high places, covering up all manner of horrors.

In the end, I realised it was time to stop theorising and put it all behind me. I was never going to find out, so perhaps my time would be better spent giving some thought to my current situation. I wasn't thinking just about this version of me, who would be back off to the 2020s soon. I was more concerned with the version of me that I was going to leave behind. What was his life going to be like? Now I had completed my mission at the school there was no real reason for me to stay there. Was it fair for me to leave that other me having to endure the next five years at Wolfminster?

I toyed with the idea of telling Mum that going there had been a mistake and that I wanted to go to St Jacobs instead. But the more I thought about that, the more I realised that it was too late to change course now. I had been effectively ostracised by my peer group in the village and had only managed to avoid physical harm at the hands of my former friends through the help of the bracelet. Somehow, I could not see them welcoming me back into the fold with open arms.

To them, I was the precocious child who thought he was above them. If I quit Wolfminster to join St Jacobs at this stage, it could get even worse. I would now be the kid who had gone to the posh school, couldn't hack it, and had come back with his tail between his legs. That would be utterly humiliating. No, it was too late. I had made my bed, and both this and the other version of me would just have to lie in it.

In addition, it would disappoint Mum. Her art career was soaring, and she had been thrilled to receive an invitation to appear in a BBC2 documentary in November. She never stopped talking about how important it was to make something of your life and what a great opportunity I had been given with the scholarship to Wolfminster. She hoped that someday I would emulate her success in whatever field I chose. I'm not sure that working in a shop by the age of eighteen was quite what she had in mind. That was what I had ended up doing before but perhaps, in much altered circumstances, things might work out differently this time.

I had spent many years in that first timeline mourning my mother as well as resenting my school, the people in it, and all it stood for. I didn't have a best friend like Maeve for support, either. Instead, I had Tracy, playing the part of wicked stepmother to perfection.

So, in the space of my time here, I had already improved my life on at least three fronts. Perhaps in this more agreeable reality, I could make better use of my time at Wolfminster. There was no denying the doors it could open, even if I hadn't been born with a silver spoon in my mouth. Staying there meant turning a blind eye to the shadowy undertones that the whole Kendrick affair had uncovered, but perhaps that was no bad thing.

If I spent the next five years trying to expose more dark secrets, I might very well end up wearing concrete boots myself. There was no way of knowing what these people might be capable of. Disposing of a child to protect themselves? I wouldn't put it past them.

I had no desire to be another Jonty or Julian. People cut from their cloth appalled me. But the school offered an incredible educational opportunity for me to tap into. Apart from the Latin, obviously. They could keep that. There was no denying the academic credentials of the teaching staff, even if it did come with an unhealthy dose of violence.

My decision was made. I would stay, and despite all the things I despised about the place, I would make the most of the opportunity and put my talents to good use. I was still incredibly gifted in mathematics, even if my progress had stalled a little in the last couple of years at my first school. I would throw all my efforts into the subject and see where it took me.

It sounded like a sensible approach but much was dependent on the version of me I left behind. I had no idea if he was going to remember any of this. If he couldn't, it would render all these plans redundant.

I wish I had asked Keith all about this when he had given me the bracelet, but it had all been very sudden at the time. I hadn't thought about any of the long-term implications back then.

I was certainly pondering them in detail now but all the paradoxes and possibilities were hard to get my head around. There was also the question of what would happen when I did return to the future. What sort of life would I have then? How would I adapt, and what would happen to the version of me I would replace when I got there? The more I thought about it, the more complicated it seemed.

I confided in Maeve, and she vowed that she would ensure she was around in forty years to help me when I got back. That was a lot to promise because it was half a lifetime away, and who knew where life might take either of us in the interim.

She also promised to help the other me here when I left him behind. As she rightly pointed out, it was in her interests as much as mine because she didn't want to lose me as a friend. Both our lives had been enhanced by finding each other in this new timeline, and neither of us wanted the growing bond between us to end.

I didn't want any of it to end. The more I thought about things, the more the same thought haunted my mind. In a nutshell, I didn't want to go back to 2021.

I wanted to stay here, with Maeve.

December 1981

As I moved into the last month of the year, I was in an increasingly reflective mood.

Over the past eleven months, I had achieved a great deal but couldn't help thinking it was odd that I was the one who had been chosen to be the custodian of the bracelet for the year.

The things I had done had been momentous in my small corner of the world but amounted to very little in the grand scheme of things. 1981 had been a tumultuous year across Britain, with soaring unemployment, civil unrest, and an economy that had been plunged into recession. It was doom and gloom all around, according to the news, but none of this impinged on the cosy little world of Meadowbrook Lane. If whoever had created the bracelet had seriously intended to give the world a helping hand, would it not have been more useful on the wrist of someone influential?

From a purely selfish point of view, I wasn't complaining. It hadn't all been plain sailing and I had suffered many sleepless nights worrying about how things were going to turn out. I'd experienced numerous beatings at the hands of friends, uncles, and masters, many caused by the actions the bracelet had directed me to take. But those physical punishments were a small price to pay weighed against the positive outcomes. Now, I was entering the final furlong, and I wasn't quite finished with my good deeds yet.

The weather turned exceptionally cold in the second week of December, indeed as bitter as I can ever remember. I was gladder than ever of the store of logs I had chopped and stockpiled during the autumn which were now keeping our fires ablaze all day as the snow began to fall. My mother said it was the coldest winter since 1963, and I could well believe it as I watched frost form on the inside of my bedroom window at night. We might have had cosy fires downstairs but there was no central heating upstairs.

Within a few days everything was frozen solid, including Stan's outside toilet, according to William. I overheard him telling my mother that he and Edna had gone cap in hand to him and Jackie asking if they could use theirs. Thank goodness we didn't live next door to them. I didn't imagine that going into the bathroom after Stan was a very pleasant experience.

Both the schools in the village closed but mine did not. On the first morning that we woke up to heavy snow, we put Radio Oxford on and listened as one school after another announced that it was closing its doors. Yet, maddeningly, there was no mention of Wolfminster. So I was forced to trudge through the drifts, freshly laid snow crunching underfoot, to the bus stop.

It was a fraught journey on roads that were barely passable but somehow the bus slithered its way slowly into the city. I ended up being fifteen minutes late for chapel, earning a whack around the head from Rasputin. When I attempted to explain about the weather I was given a lecture about Wolfminster boys keeping a stiff upper lip, along with some rubbish about it not deterring Scott on his Antarctic expedition. I refrained from pointing out that it hadn't done Scott any good, because to have done so would have only invited further punishment.

I found out later that we were the only school open in Oxfordshire that day, so while I was shivering and reciting Latin verbs in a freezing classroom, every other child in the county was out building snowmen and racing down hills on bin bags.

My next errand of mercy came in the form of a rescue mission after school. After a hair-raising ride home on the bus, along a road that had barely defrosted all day, the bracelet flashed red, and into my head popped a suggestion that I should take a different route home.

I wasn't keen because it was out of my way in Baltic conditions, and darkness had already fallen. I was in danger of slipping over with every step, and my teeth were chattering from the cold. One of Wolfminster's most unbelievably stupid rules was that pupils were not allowed to wear coats. We were representing the school at all times which meant that our blazer and tie must always be on display. When one kid complained to Remus about this, the sadistic old git's response was to make him remove his gloves and do twenty press-ups in the snow.

I hadn't managed to warm up since leaving school because the bus didn't appear to possess any sort of heating system. So being urged by the bracelet to go miles out of my way on the walk home did not go down well, especially as it hadn't indicated the reason why.

Originally, I surmised that it might be to avoid trouble with Martin and his over-growing gang of thugs, but instead it directed me through the front gate into the garden of one of the cottages on the other side of the village. There I found none other than old Mrs Walters, the lady who had got lucky when Art had turned up at the carnival. She had fallen over and collapsed in the snow, standard-issue old-person tartan shopping trolley upended beside her. I could see if she didn't get help fast, she would expire from hypothermia.

I raised the alarm, the neighbours rallied around to help, and paramedics were called. My timely intervention did the trick, and Mrs Walters lived to fight another day.

It was almost 5 o'clock, and pitch dark by the time I got home. As I stepped through the front door I was dismayed to hear Edith rabbiting on about the weather. Just what I didn't need after a long, cold day.

"I tell you, Mary, this is going to be the coldest winter since 1947. I said when all the birds migrated early this autumn it was going to be a bad one."

"I thought 1963 was worse," replied Mum. "That went on for months."

"Ah, but we didn't have the snow then, like we did in '47. Up to the bedroom windows it was. Don't you remember? We built a tunnel from the farmhouse to the barn."

Ordinarily, I would have gone straight upstairs to avoid her but my fingers were practically turning blue with the cold and all I could think about was that big roaring fire in the kitchen. I find it incredibly boring when people bang on incessantly about the weather but nothing was keeping me from the warmth a moment longer.

"Oh, Nick, have you been having fun in the snow?" asked Edith, as I dropped my satchel in the corner and made a beeline for the flames.

"Hardly," I replied. "I've been at school. That's why I'm wearing my uniform."

"Pity," she said. "Simon and the others have been up on Beacon Hill sledging all day."

"Why are you so late?" asked Mum.

"I've been doing a good turn," I replied. "Old Mrs Walters fell over in the snow and I, along with a few others, helped her."

"Good for you," she replied. "It's looking lethal out there. Aunt Edith thinks we're going to get a white Christmas."

"We're long overdue one," said Edith. "When I was a girl, we had a white Christmas every year."

This was a blatant untruth, and I was tempted to call her out on it but what would be the point? She would only get cross and I didn't have the facts and figures at my disposal to disprove her.

Perhaps she didn't know she was wrong and was reimagining her youth through rose-coloured spectacles. Or maybe Bing Crosby was to blame, for planting the idea in her head. Whatever the reason, she was wrong. True white Christmases were once-in-a-lifetime events, at least where we lived, in the south Midlands. Perhaps they had them more often up north.

They ought not to be so rare. There had been plenty of snowy winters during my lifetime but the whiteouts never came at the right time. Occasionally there was a year with a sleety shower, or a few bits of dirty melting snow left over from a few days before. But I had never seen what I would deem to be a proper white Christmas.

By that, I mean when it starts snowing after dark on Christmas Eve, and then there's a pristine white blanket covering everything the next morning. I don't believe it was any different in the past, and I'm sure weather statistics would back me up. But without the numbers to hand I would have to just put up with listening to Edith talking out of her arse until she got bored and went home.

Unfortunately, her reminiscences of the festive seasons of the past did not end with the weather as she continued to bang on about Christmases past, coming out with one dubious claim after another.

"And there was none of this commercialisation you get nowadays. People used to put their tree up on Christmas Eve and no one even talked about Christmas before then. As for presents, you were grateful for what you were given. Me and Carol had one tangerine between us one year before you were born, and we made it last all week."

This continued for some time, with Mum nodding and acknowledging without offering much in the way of responses. She knew it was all bollocks just as much as I did, so I sat warming my hands in front of the fire until Edith finally relented and left, about fifteen minutes after my arrival.

"Thank God for that," I said. "I thought she would never go. What was she doing here?"

"She just came to talk about arrangements for Christmas."

"Which is two weeks away," I said. "So much for nobody talking about it until Christmas Eve. And I don't know what there is to talk about anyway. We do the same thing every year. What's for tea?"

"Casserole," she said.

"I thought so," I said, having smelt the aromas of beef, onion and red wine pervading the kitchen as soon as I had come in. I was going to miss all these wonderful meals when I went back to my own time. I never seemed to have the time or the inclination to emulate my mother in the kitchen when I became an adult.

The cold snap deepened by the weekend with record low temperatures being recorded across the country, as low as minus twenty in places. It was shaping up to be the coldest December of the century but at least I was to be spared any more school. Even Wolfminster had to admit defeat and close on Monday 14th, and with term due to end the next day, there were thankfully no more snowy treks to Oxford. St Jacob's, however, did reopen for a couple of days at the end of that week as they didn't finish until Friday. Still, it remained so cold that I began to wonder if there would be snow at Christmas after all, even though I didn't remember it.

Just before Christmas, there was an incredibly tragic event in the news. The weather wasn't just cold, it was stormy too, especially around the coasts. I was shocked when news came in of the capsizing of the Penlee lifeboat off the coast of Cornwall with the loss of all hands. Surely this was the sort of thing the bracelet should have been designed to prevent, so why didn't it?

The unforgiving seas around Britain had claimed thousands of vessels over the centuries, and that fateful night was no exception. The bracelet couldn't change the weather but if the stricken vessel that the lifeboat had gone to rescue had not set sail in the first place, none of it would have happened. But it seemed it could not, or would not, get involved, just as it hadn't saved the plane that had gone down on the way to New York.

Saving Mrs Walters turned out to be the final task the bracelet had for me. But there were still decisions to be made about the future, including one which was sprung on me unexpectedly on Christmas Eve.

That morning, Mum sent me into the village to pick up our turkey from the butcher. We did not have to pay for this because of the eggs we supplied him throughout the year for him to sell in his shop. This was the way our little rural world still worked in 1981, with the trade and barter economy still thriving.

By sending me, Mum could concentrate on baking a batch of sausage rolls in preparation for the first of the Christmas family gatherings, at Edith's that evening. But when I got back there wasn't much baking going on. Mum was sitting at the far end of the kitchen table, and seated opposite was someone I hadn't expected to ever see here again.

As my father greeted me with a weary, "Hello, Nick," I couldn't help but notice the decline in him. His once meticulous appearance was now dishevelled, his hair was un-brushed, and his clothes creased and unkempt. He hadn't shaved, either. Even Stan and Dennis didn't look as bad as this.

But it was the weariness etched into his features, notably the shadows beneath his eyes, that gave the clearest indication that all was not well in his world.

None of this generated any sympathy from me. I suspected what had probably happened because I had seen it coming. It didn't take long to get the confirmation.

"What's he doing here?" I asked, turning towards my mother. Seated at opposite ends of the table as they were, they looked like two world leaders at a peace summit. I hoped that wasn't what this was.

"Tracy's dumped him," she said. "He says he's got nowhere else to go."

Just as I had predicted. What a bloody fool he was.

"What happened?" I asked, directly to him this time.

"I'd rather not say," he said, eyes angled down at the table in embarrassment. He didn't need to say anything. I knew enough about the kind of girl Tracy was to have figured it out. But Mum had no qualms about filling in the blanks, knowing she didn't need to sugar-coat it for my benefit.

"He came home early and found Tracy in bed with their landlord, who promptly threw him out."

"Mary, don't tell the boy that," said Dad. "He's too young to be hearing about that sort of thing."

"Oh, I think you'll find Nick's a lot more mature than you might think. You know, you've got a hell of a check coming crawling back here. Do you honestly think I'm going to take you back after all you've done?"

"It's not just about us, though, is it? What about the boy? He needs both his parents."

She paused, a thoughtful look on her face. Was she wavering? It looked that way, as she turned to me to seek my opinion.

"I don't know. What do you think, Nick?"

She had handed the decision to me. What was the right thing to do? I'm sure if I had looked down at the bracelet it might have indicated the best answer to give but I wasn't reciting a Latin verb here. This was a personal choice which I was going to make on my own. I averted my gaze from my arm and weighed things up. It didn't take long.

"We don't need him," I said with conviction. "He betrayed us before. If he can do it once, he can do it again."

"That's what I think too," she said. "But I probably would have taken him back for your sake if you had begged me."

"Well, I'm begging you not to."

"Please, Nick," he pleaded, rather pathetically. "I can change. I'll never do it again. I care about you, honestly. Look, I've even brought you a present, see?"

I hadn't paid any attention to the badly wrapped rectangular box on the table which he now pushed towards me. It didn't even have proper gift wrap on it, just some blue crêpe paper that looked suspiciously like the stuff that Peter Dominic wrapped their bottles of wine in.

"I know it's a day early but you can open it now. That's OK, isn't it, Mary?"

"I suppose so."

He handed me the box, which I reluctantly took, and tore off the blue paper. It was a ZX81.

"You wanted one of those, didn't you?"

"I've already got one. Mum bought me one for my birthday. Which you would have known if you had bothered to show the slightest bit of interest in me over the past six months. So why don't you just go?"

"I've got nowhere to go."

"Sure you have. What about Grandma Taylor?"

"But she's in Reading," he protested

"Then if you catch a train you can be there before dark," said Mum. "She's always saying how little she sees of you. Now's your chance."

I knew my father didn't get on with his mother, but it seemed he was going to have to.

"The thing is, I'm a little short on cash. I spent what I had on this computer. I don't suppose…"

"I'll give you the money for the train fare," she said. "Where did you buy that from?"

"Dixons, in Oxford."

"I suggest you take it back and ask for a refund before you catch the train. Unless you want to give it to your mother, but I'm not sure octogenarians are into that sort of thing."

"So that's it, then?" he asked.

"That's it," she said, and to emphasise that I echoed her sentiment, I moved to stand behind her at the far end of the table.

And that was the last I saw of him, in 1981 anyway. With that uncomfortable conversation behind me, I resolved to make the most of my final week without worrying about my imminent departure.

That meant three days in a row on the Christmas circuit, beginning with the gathering at Edith's at which I once again had to endure being smothered in lipstick and perfume by Carol, while the men compared whiskies and talked about cars.

Christmas Day dawned with not a snowflake in sight, just a few slushy leftovers, including a very sorry-looking snowman that Maeve and I had made over a week earlier. Originally about five feet tall, it had now been reduced to a football-sized lump with a mouldy carrot and a couple of pieces of coal sitting atop. It could barely be seen from my bedroom window through the thick fog that had descended on the lane.

Maeve came round to give me my Christmas present which I was delighted to discover was the album *Dare* by The Human League. This year, there was a decent Christmas number one for a change. The annual race for the festive top spot had been overwhelmingly disappointing during my lifetime, with very few decent records taking the prize. Most years, it ended up being a charity single, a dreary ballad, the winner of a TV talent show, or some dreadful novelty record like Mr Blobby.

The early part of this decade was particularly bad, with this year sandwiched between St Winifred's School Choir in 1980 and Renée and Renato in 1982. Thankfully, The Human League came to the rescue in 1981, and as Britain shivered they climbed to the summit with 'Don't You Want Me?' It's an overused tag, I know, but to me, the song truly is a classic. It's hard to believe it was over forty years ago.

I had been enthusing about it and playing the single nonstop all through December so it was no surprise that Maeve bought me the album. In return, I got her *The Best of Blondie* on cassette which was equally well received. And from now on, I would be able to play cassettes too, as my mother had generously given me a Sony Walkman which was still a new thing in 1981. Hardly anyone had got one yet, not even James Spencer, the kid who had everything. To older me, the Walkman was old hat, yet I still enjoyed playing around with the old technology.

The retro fun also applied to one of my other presents, the game *3D Monster Maze* for the ZX81, which William and Jackie had bought me for Christmas. I loaded it up just for a laugh. Every time I played one of the games on this computer, I marvelled at how I used to think these primitive offerings were state-of-the-art. After twice crashing during the laborious loading process, due to the dreaded RAM pack wobble that afflicted this temperamental machine, I got it up and running.

As it turned out, I found the blocky, slow-moving black-and-white graphics rather fun and spent a good hour being chased around by a T-Rex which had the letter 'O' for its eyes, and teeth represented by the letter 'V'. Even so, I had to hand it to these early game designers. They did an amazing job with the incredibly limited resources at their disposal.

Then, it was time for the centrepiece of the Cartwright family Christmas – dinner at the farmhouse.

Nellie was no longer up to cooking a grand meal for four families so we had developed a system where we all chipped in. My mother cooked a turkey, Jackie prepared a goose, and Edith made a leg of pork. Trust her to get the cheapest cut.

They prepared these in their own kitchens, while Carol would come over and help Nellie prepare all the trimmings at the farmhouse. A feature of the large kitchen on the farm was that it still had a massive wrought iron stove from the early twentieth century, designed for the large family that had lived there at the time. While the cooking was in full flow, my three uncles decamped to the pub.

Once it was all ready we took everything up to the farm, wrapped in silver foil, ready for the grand feast, which this year was for twelve of us, three less than the previous year. In addition to the absence of Dad and Tracy, my sister was also missing, having decided to spend the holidays in Australia.

Edith remarked ruefully that this was the lowest number she could remember at a Cartwright Christmas dinner since she was born. She raised concerns that family ties were not what they used to be and that this annual gathering was in danger of dying out. For once, she had a point. My memory from the old timeline was that this tradition fizzled out soon after my mother's death as Tracy couldn't be bothered to contribute, and William had refused to be in the same room as her or my father. The tradition began to fall apart, and with Jack and Nellie passing on within a few years that was the end of it.

This time, I hoped things would turn out differently. I said as much to Mum in a quiet moment later in the afternoon. By then most of the older members of the family were snoozing off their lunch on the sofa, or in Nellie's case, her favourite rocking chair. That wasn't all we talked about as I warned her about some other things that might later threaten her birthright, such as the family losing the farmhouse. She assured me she would do the utmost to keep that from happening.

After a Boxing Day sortie to Boars Hill, I spent as much of the last few days as possible with some of those I was not to see again, particularly my grandparents. I was sad that I was soon to lose them for a second time, but tried to look at it positively. Most people would never have had the chance to see them again in the first place.

As for some of the others, I wouldn't miss them, particularly Dennis, who had shown himself to be a petty, small-minded sadist. I still hadn't forgiven him for what he had done to me on the day of the street party and felt no sorrow that he would be dead before the turn of the millennium.

Edith and Carol, the eldest siblings, would be gone by the time I returned too, but I had no idea about my mother. She would be in her eighties by then, nearly as old as Nellie was now. There was no guarantee she would still be with us. All I could do was hope.

The person I was going to miss the most was Maeve. She had played no part in my previous life but had become my best friend very quickly in this one. It was hard to imagine life without her. Would she still be around in 2021? I know she had promised she would be, but forty years was a long time to keep a promise.

I was confident that this time she would survive her difficult teenage years but where would life take her after that? She might end up returning to Ireland. Not wanting to say goodbye to her until the last possible moment, I persuaded Jackie to invite both her and her mother to the New Year's Eve party.

Only Maeve and Mum knew what was about to happen to me, and they were prepared to deal with whatever might occur at midnight. I tried not to think about it as the evening progressed, just savouring as much of my last night as I could.

I felt more nostalgic during this final evening than I had at any time during the past year, knowing it was all about to come to an end. For once, I didn't mind Edith's clichés, Henry's boorish snobbery, or Carol's over-affectionate embraces. It was the last time I was to see any of them.

I even found the antics of nosey Brenda and her family amusing, including when I caught her daughter Karen rummaging through the contents of the bathroom cabinet. Like mother, like daughter.

As for Brenda's dishwater-dull husband, the seldom-seen Robert, he spent the evening boring the other men with excruciating anecdotes about the minutiae of his tedious-sounding job at the local council offices. I had often wondered why we saw so little of him, even at the weekends when Brenda was out in the lane gossiping.

Was he taking sanctuary from her in his garden shed, or did she keep him locked up inside somewhere? The mind boggled. He would be dead by the time I got back to the future, but Brenda and Karen? They would probably go on forever.

As midnight approached the adults were all outrageously tipsy, courtesy of William's latest experiment, a wine fermented from beetroot. Not for the first time, I felt envious of the adults, not having been able to enjoy an alcoholic beverage for nearly a year. Under these circumstances, even William's wine looked appetising. I resolved that the first thing I was going to do when I got back was treat myself to a decent drink. Dry January? Not for me.

With a few minutes to go, Jackie flicked on the TV which was tuned into ATV. They were showing a Hogmanay-themed special. It was a historic night in television as this was the very last programme that would ever be shown on this long-running station.

In the morning it would be rebranded as a new channel called Central which would be the face of ITV in the Midlands from 1982. I remembered being disappointed when it changed as I missed the old ATV colourful circles that burst onto the screen before each programme. I recall that the new channel also stopped *Tiswas* not long afterwards, though to be fair it had probably run its course.

None of that mattered to me because I wouldn't be around to see it. As the revellers on the television, and the family around me began counting down from ten, my mother gripped my left hand tightly.

As Maeve took hold of my right, I turned to look at her one last time, and simply whispered, "Goodbye."

January 2021

As the word "goodbye" left my lips, the world blurred and shifted, before reassembling around me. The whole process took less than a second, and I recognised my new surroundings as soon as it was over.

I was in the familiar, yet much altered, living room of the farmhouse. The basic shape was as it had always been. The large arch leading through to the kitchen with its exposed brickwork and wooden beams was just as it had been the last time I visited Jack and Nellie on my final day in 1981. The fireplace, crackling away to keep out the winter chill, was also unchanged.

The layout of the room might not have changed but the décor certainly had. Gone were the rough, basic furnishings of the past. Two sumptuous leather sofas now took up the space previously occupied by the threadbare couch and rickety rocking chairs of my grandparents. Plush velvet curtains framed the windows, while the walls were a rich cream colour, adorned with paintings that bore the unmistakable mark of my mother's artistic talent.

A flat-screen television in the corner was showing high definition pictures of Big Ben striking midnight, confirming that I was back in my own time.

I absorbed all these details in an instant, before registering the comforting grip of two hands. For a moment I thought I had somehow dragged Maeve and Mum through time with me but as I looked down, I could see the hand to my left was weathered and wrinkled. My gaze shifted upwards, and there was Mum, her eighty-two-year-old eyes still bright with life despite the passage of time.

The hand on my right was smoother, younger, and adorned with a gold band on the fourth finger. I looked up to see Maeve, now fully-grown and radiant with her familiar red curls cascading down to her shoulders. I glanced back to my left hand to see that I too wore a wedding ring. I didn't even need to ask because I instinctively knew it. We were married. Of course we were. It made perfect sense.

"Are you…?" Maeve began, her voice filled with a mix of hope and uncertainty.

"Back?" I finished, taking in the scene before me. Across the room, three young figures lounged on one of the leather sofas, their faces a blend of curiosity and amusement as they peered at me. I felt a familiarity with them that I couldn't quite place, before adding, "Yes, I'm back."

"Just as we expected," she said, giving my hand a squeeze of reassurance. "How much do you remember?"

"Nothing since 1981," I confessed, my gaze lingering on the trio before me. If Maeve and I were married, then these must be…

My train of thought was interrupted as the boy in the middle of the sofa piped up. "Phew, that's a relief. If he doesn't remember anything, does that mean I'm not grounded anymore?"

He looked to be in his late teens, with bright blue eyes which sparkled with mischief as he spoke, adding a playful edge to his words. He had sandy blond hair which was tousled in small curls, the same shape as

Maeve's, and was sitting between two girls, one older, one younger.

"You couldn't go anywhere, even if you wanted to," retorted the younger girl on the right, who had inherited Maeve's red hair. She had striking green eyes, full of energy, suggesting a razor-sharp mind. "We're in tier three, remember?"

Of course, tier three. I had forgotten all about the coronavirus and the restrictions in the year I had been away. Perhaps that was why there was no one else here other than us six. They were all in their own homes in their household bubbles.

"Are you alright, Dad?" asked the older blonde girl on the other side, with genuine concern.

Dad. Something I had never been called before. This was going to take a bit of getting used to.

"He doesn't remember, do you, darling?" said Maeve, her voice soft, which reassured me that she knew all about what I was going through. "But he will."

"He did last time," said Mum, who had by now let go of my hand. "It just takes a couple of days."

"I bet he doesn't even know who we are!" said the boy, a mischievous twinkle in his eye. "Hey, Dad, I lent you fifty quid yesterday. Can I have it back?"

He chuckled before the younger girl cut him down to size.

"Adam, stop taking the piss out of Dad," she scolded. "Or I'll tell him why you were grounded."

All of this was said light-heartedly, suggesting we were a family at ease with each other. It felt far more natural than family interactions had been in 1981 when the likes of Edith and Dennis were around. Despite my memory loss, I could feel a sense of belonging that comes with being part of a close-knit family. It was still a little disorienting with the amnesia, though.

"I think I'd better do some introductions," said Maeve, sensing that I was a little overwhelmed by the occasion. "Nick, congratulations. You're a father. Meet Andrea, Adam, and Siobhan."

"This is ridiculous," said Adam, "You're not serious about all this, are you? He hasn't really travelled in time. This is just some big prank you boomers have dreamt up. Now, aren't we going to wish each other all a happy New Year?"

There was a chorus of greetings between us as 'Auld Lang Syne' rang out from the television, before Maeve said, "You'd better be glad he did travel back in time. Because if he hadn't, none of you lot would ever have existed. Oh, and for your information, we're not boomers. We're Generation X – the best generation that ever lived, and don't you forget it!"

"Whatever," said Adam. "When are we opening the champagne?"

"Gosh, I'd forgotten all about the champagne," said Maeve, dashing off through the arch to the kitchen, calling back, "Hang on a sec…"

She returned with a bottle and six glasses, allowing us to properly toast the New Year. It was the first proper drink I'd had for a year and I savoured every drop. From what I'd seen so far, this homecoming truly was a cause for celebration.

I still felt a little weird, as if I were an outsider crashing someone's party but from what had been said, I was confident it would all come flooding back. In the meantime, there were a million questions I wanted to ask but I decided they could wait until Maeve and I were alone together.

That moment came about an hour and a half later when we made our way up to the master bedroom. All six of us now lived in the farmhouse which I had been relieved to find had no longer been turned into an old folks' home. Mum had kept her promise. I had no time to think about that now though, because as soon as we were alone, Maeve started kissing me passionately, which was the prelude to us making love. This was for me, devoid of memories, effectively our first time.

Afterwards, we cuddled up and talked all night, as she filled me in on everything that had happened in the past forty years.

She explained that immediately after I had left, I had forgotten everything. It was as if my entire memory of the time I had spent in 1981 had been wiped, with my response to Maeve when she turned and said, "Happy New Year," being, "Who are you?"

Maeve and Mum had been very concerned about me, especially as I seemed to have lost all my memories from 1981. I didn't even know that I now went to Wolfminster. Thankfully, the amnesia proved to be only temporary. Over the following few days, my mind was repopulated with the knowledge of everything that had happened that year, merging with my existing memories from my younger years.

Interestingly, the restored me had not retained any knowledge of my previous timeline from 1982 onwards. I had known that I had come back to the past to do the things I had done but I couldn't remember why. This also applied to future world events, about which I knew nothing.

We discussed why this might be, concluding that perhaps, other than for the year when in possession of the bracelet, it would not be good for any individual to keep their knowledge of the future. Even if they were scrupulous enough not to use it to their advantage, it could be a curse rather than a blessing.

Who would want to be burdened with the knowledge of future disasters, terrorist attacks, and all the other bad things that go on in the world? Free from fretting about such things, custodians of the bracelet would be able to go back to living a perfectly normal life. Which is exactly, it seems, what I had done.

Maeve and I remained firm friends, facing the challenges of the world together, and keeping at bay those who desired to make our teenage lives a misery. By the time we both turned sixteen, we had fallen in love. There was never any question of there being anyone else for either of us. We married in 1995, with our firstborn, Andrea, arriving three years later, followed by Adam in 2002, and Siobhan in 2003.

Maeve had relished being a mother, enjoying every minute of bringing up the children. She had done this in tandem with running a successful online fashion business, where she designed quirky and unusual outfits with a Celtic flair. She had built up a loyal and devoted clientele of folky and hippy types who were always looking for something outside the mainstream to wear to parties and festivals.

It was after 6am by the time we got to sleep, by which time I was in a very happy place. I'd had to absorb a lot of information in a very short time but it was all positive. By the following afternoon my memories were beginning to return, and within a couple of days, as Maeve had suggested, they had all come back. I had a whole new lifetime of experiences to think about. How did my new life compare with my old one?

The second time around, I had tackled the challenges of Wolfminster with gusto, just as I had planned. Rekindling my earlier love of mathematics, I stayed the full seven years, leading to a first-class degree from Oxford, and then a lucrative career in finance.

I had never gone into retail which meant some people who had featured in my past life never played a part in this one. I can't say I was sad about most of them, my two ex-wives for a start. Being with Maeve spared both me and them all that heartbreak that had gone before.

Thomas Scott, my old friend and colleague, was a different matter. We had been through a lot together, and knowing our paths had never crossed did fill me with sadness. I thought about the impact I'd had on his life and how things might have turned out for him.

There was one event I was particularly curious about. In 1998, we had gone to Ibiza and got caught up in an incident when his future wife had been kidnapped. It had been up to the two of us to save her but in the new timeline, I hadn't been involved. How had that turned out without me? I didn't want anything I'd done to have prevented them from being together. Thomas and Sarah had been my two best friends in my old life, in which they were extremely happy together.

I was determined to find out so I looked him up on social media. I was happy to discover that the two of them, along with their daughter Stacey, were living happily together in Oxford. It was a great relief. Perhaps another friend had filled in my role on the holiday. Unless I befriended Thomas and asked, I guess I would never know.

And what about that first interaction with the Diamond Geezer? I thought about him giving me the bracelet at the hospital. In this timeline, I hadn't been there because my father was still alive. So how could he have given me the bracelet? Maeve and I tried to figure out this paradox but after a while realised we were going around in circles and that it wasn't worth worrying about it. Things had turned out well for us, so there was no point getting hung up on the technicalities.

Dad had gone to live in Reading for a while in the 1980s but had returned to the village after Grandma Taylor had died, found a place to live, and rebuilt his business. He had eventually remarried, to a retired accountant, and was living happily with her in a house in the village. It seemed that a life without Tracy had been beneficial, at least when it came to life expectancy. His interactions with the family were at least now civil, though William had never fully forgiven him.

He and Jackie were alive, and still living in Fuchsia but Tracy had never returned. The ever-present Brenda was also still in situ. As for the other cottages, they had all been bought by us, keeping them out of the hands of second-homeowners and wealthy commuters.

Mum had enjoyed a stellar career in the art world. In addition to her painting, she also became something of a minor celebrity in the 1980s, presenting arts programmes on both the BBC and the fledgling Channel 4. Her success was the reason we were living in the farmhouse now.

With her money, there was no need to sell off the family seat, though it no longer operated as a fully functioning farm. She did eventually agree to sell off some of the land to a local building firm, recognising the need for new housing for local people, but we retained half a dozen acres.

On this land we still grew a few vegetables, maintained a small orchard, and kept chickens. In addition, William had started his own winemaking business in the barn. He had become surprisingly adept, considering his early dubious attempts, and had even won a couple of awards. He was happily doing this, even in his eighties, and was still experimenting away, claiming he hadn't found a fruit or vegetable yet that he couldn't make wine out of.

Mum and I moved into the farmhouse after Jack and Nellie died. With five bedrooms, there was plenty of room for Maeve and the children when they came along. We kept Wisteria and rented it out, usually to local families. We all agreed how important it was to keep a sense of community in the lane. After Edith, Dennis, Stan, and Edna were all gone, we were able to buy up Rosemary and Honeysuckle. Maeve's mother now lived in one of them rent-free.

The long-term plan was that we would keep all of these properties for Andrea, Adam, and Siobhan, all of whom would one day have a home waiting for them when the time came to start families of their own.

Mum was determined that in an increasingly fragmented world where many families scattered to the four corners of the globe, the same wasn't going to happen to us. It was a pity my sister didn't see it that way. We saw Linda once a year if we were lucky.

With my memories intact, I slipped easily into my new life, making the most of the opportunity to spend as much time as possible with the family. A new national lockdown was announced a few days into January, which meant I was going to be working online from home for the foreseeable future.

Adam was in a similar boat, informed that he wouldn't be going back to Plymouth where he was studying music but spending the term working at home. The schools were also shut, leaving Siobhan confined to base too, and with Andrea furloughed, we spent the first few months of 2021 cosily tucked up together, enjoying family nights in front of the fire.

It was the sort of life I could never have imagined before. There was a lot of banter, plenty of laughs, and many family in-jokes. We were all so comfortable with each other that no one ever had to "mind their Ps and Qs" as Edith used to say.

It couldn't have been more different to the lousy life I'd had growing up with Dad and Tracy, followed by decades of failed relationships and loneliness. My whole world had been rewritten, predominantly by changing the course of one pivotal event. And, it had all been down to the bracelet. There had been times I had despised it, but it had all come good in the end. Looking at what I had now, I knew that I wouldn't change a thing.

The device on my arm had gone inert now. It would remain in hibernation on my wrist until the end of the year when it would be time to pass it on to a new recipient.

Who would it choose next, I wondered?

THE END – for now, but you can meet the next recipient of the bracelet in 1982: A Year in the Life of Wendy Wood.

Also by Jason Ayres
1980: A Year in the Life of Keith Diamond

Relive the 1980s in this rip-roaring time travel adventure from bestselling author, Jason Ayres.

As the 2020s dawn, Keith Diamond, the self-styled 'Diamond Geezer', works as a shock jock presenter at controversial radio station, ChatFM. When the station comes under new management, Keith finds himself surplus to requirements. His employment prospects look bleak until a stranger gives him a bracelet that catapults him forty years back in time to when he was a young journalist. Soaking up the culture, Keith immerses himself in the music scene, going to see legendary bands like The Clash, Blondie, and The Specials, but soon there are more important tasks at hand.

Working in Fleet Street, Keith finds himself thrust into the news stories of the day. These range from the hunt for the Yorkshire Ripper to the death of John Lennon, plus the world's obsession with "Who Shot JR?" From a personal perspective, 1980 is a pivotal year on which both his and many of his friends' destinies depend. Can he rectify past mistakes, avert disasters, and reshape both his future and that of others?

Join Keith, as he revisits the culture and events of 1980, in this humorous and thought-provoking time travel story.

UK: https://www.amazon.co.uk/dp/B0CN3VY6TJ/
US: https://www.amazon.com/dp/B0CN3VY6TJ/

Also by Jason Ayres
1982: A Year in the Life of Wendy Wood

Meet Wendy Wood. The popstar that never was…

In 1982, Wendy Wood was poised on the brink of stardom. Lead singer with talented local band, Velvet Temptation, she was a rising star of the Oxford music scene. Tipped for fame by the music press, success seemed inevitable.

But conflict within the band, a series of betrayals and infidelities, and an unwelcome run of bad luck all played a part in shattering her dreams.

Forty years later, her health failing, Wendy's only comfort is in karaoke nights, where every song is a poignant reminder of what might have been.

Then, out of the blue, she's handed the means to return to the past. Determined to rewrite her destiny, Wendy is steadfast in her pursuit of the fame that once slipped through her fingers.

Join Wendy as she immerses herself in the vibrant music scene of 1982, navigating the complexities of love, ambition, and second chances in this thought-provoking time travel story.

UK: https://www.amazon.co.uk/dp/B0CW1HDT72
US: https://www.amazon.com/dp/B0CW1HDT72

The Time Bubble Collection

The Time Bubble is an epic series, exploring time travel from every possible angle:

1) The Time Bubble
2) Global Cooling
3) Man Out of Time
4) Splinters in Time
5) Class of '92
6) Vanishing Point
7) Midlife Crisis
8) Rock Bottom
9) My Tomorrow, Your Yesterday
10) Happy New Year
11) Return to Tomorrow
12) Cause of Death
13) Lauren's Odyssey
14) Gone to the Rapture
15) Closing Time

UK Link:

https://www.amazon.co.uk/Jason-Ayres/e/B00CQO4XJC/

US Link:

https://www.amazon.com/Jason-Ayres/e/B00CQO4XJC/

Also by Jason Ayres
The Time Bubble

Time travel fans will love this fresh new approach to the genre - the first in an epic series by bestselling author Jason Ayres.

The story begins with the discovery of the very first Time Bubble beneath a railway line, kicking off a life-changing series of adventures.

At first, it's just a bit of fun, jumping a few seconds into the future. Soon things take a more serious turn as the leaps in time increase in duration. When a teenage girl goes missing, and the police become involved, suspicion falls on her boyfriend. How can he explain where she is? Will anyone believe him?

The Time Bubble is the first part of a hugely popular series (over 100,000 copies sold) exploring the time travel genre in original and innovative ways. The novels follow the main characters from youth to middle age as they jump forwards, backwards, and sideways into alternate worlds.

UK: https://www.amazon.co.uk/dp/B00L3K1B8G
US: https://www.amazon.com/dp/B00L3K1B8G

The Ronnie and Bernard Adventures

The Ronnie and Bernard Adventures are a pair of humorous novels with mild science fiction and horror elements set in the 1970s. The stories follow the fortunes of two actors from very different backgrounds.

Together they tackle mysteries, travel in time, and negotiate the rocky path of life as jobbing actors, from daytime soaps to panto.

Anyone who remembers the 1970s will love these nostalgic stories looking back at a time when life was simpler, and the world didn't take itself too seriously. Packed with period detail, humour, and references to the era, they are the perfect antidote to modern living.

1) The Crooked Line
2) The Haunted Theatre

UK Link:

https://www.amazon.co.uk/Jason-Ayres/e/B0BR9SMPPY/

US Link:

https://www.amazon.com/Jason-Ayres/e/B0BR9SMPPY/

Follow the Author

To ensure you never miss a release, or to be informed of special deals on Amazon, sign up to follow me on my author page which can be found here:

https://www.amazon.co.uk/stores/Jason-Ayres/author/B00CQO4XJC

For exclusive content from me, regular newsletters and occasional freebies and offers, sign up to my mailing list here:

https://www.jasonayres.co.uk/contact/ or email me directly: jason.ayres@btinternet.com

And of course, there is Facebook, X, and YouTube!

https://www.facebook.com/TheTimeBubble/

https://twitter.com/TheTimeBubble/

https://www.youtube.com/channel/UCg13jmfTUTFCqWWZrPmXqJQ

Finally, if you loved this book and have the time to leave a star rating or review on Amazon, it is always hugely appreciated!